力得文化
Leader Culture

Lead your way. Be your own leader!

力得文化
Leader Culture

Lead your way. Be your own leader!

力得文化
Leader Culture

解密中英互譯技巧

黃瀅瑄 (Sandra Huang) ◎ 著

Decoding
English & Chinese
Translation

翻譯+英文寫作 能力一次躍進！

特別收錄

【前輩指點】分享譯者前輩的接案親身經歷和入行小叮嚀，避免踩到翻譯這一行的地雷！

新鮮人入行必備寶典，老手必藏翻譯訣竅！

一次解開一定要知道的中英互譯2大密碼，晉升自己的翻譯功力！

Code 1【熟練翻譯技巧】 翻譯不是一般人所想的直接照字面翻，透過閱讀翻譯技巧理論與延伸應用的實例，讓譯文擁有「信、達、雅」的專業程度！

信 可信度，符合原文的意義　達 流暢度，暢達詞意，文句通順　雅 文雅度，譯文文字優美

Code 2【抓準原文的精髓】 透過閱讀8大【廣告、藝術、觀光、商管、歷史、教育、動畫、健康】領域的範文，先了解各類文章的脈絡與屬性，再看重點句型解析快速理解原文的重點，幫助譯者在翻譯時更上手！

作者序
Author

　　其實，關於語言學習與翻譯，一直不敢說有多大深厚的內功實力累積，倒是數十年來，雖非本科班出身，但卻也沒中斷過語言學習這件事，並也在日常生活中，盡量找機會去體用它。特別是翻譯，更是一門無法有絕對定論的技巧學科，以實用性來看，只要達到了翻譯的目的，就不能說它是錯的。越是接近原作者思想，越是能將意涵想法傳達至讀者，產生共鳴，就越能算是較好的翻譯，而且同樣從事翻譯的前輩、後輩、同期們，應不會特別有人敢發霸氣豪語的說他翻的一定是正確沒問題的，從業泰半都是虛心學習，樂於經驗分享的。

　　此次，非常感謝倍斯特出版社給予機會，讓本人有幸與大家分享一點淺薄經驗，特別更感謝編輯于婷的協助，讓這本書在本人歷經流感超級病毒摧殘後，終於完成了，希望這好不容易生出來的寶貝，可以為想進入翻譯行業，或是已從事翻譯的同業後進們提供一些具參考價值又不會太艱澀難讀，一次可以接觸廣泛領域主題的各式建議譯文、譯法參考，往更專業的翻譯職涯路上前進。

黃瀅瑄 Sandra Huang

編者序
Editor

　　許多人對翻譯這個行業帶有憧憬，卻又常常不知道該怎麼入行，或是在翻譯工作上該注意什麼地方。

　　其實，中英翻譯並非一味地遵從原文，而更該是在保留原文涵義的同時，也正確地以另一種語言表達出原作者所要傳達的理念。簡言之，即是讓譯文達到「信、達、雅」的水準。

　　當一個好翻譯，最重要的就是多讀、多看、多練。除了一邊廣泛閱讀不同類型的文章，熟習不同領域的中英文用詞外，練習更是不可或缺的一部分。

　　本書前半部會簡述翻譯大概的理論，後半部則提供範例與翻譯前輩的工作經驗談，期許讀者能藉此獲得更多翻譯工作上的幫助！

編輯部

使用說明
Instructions

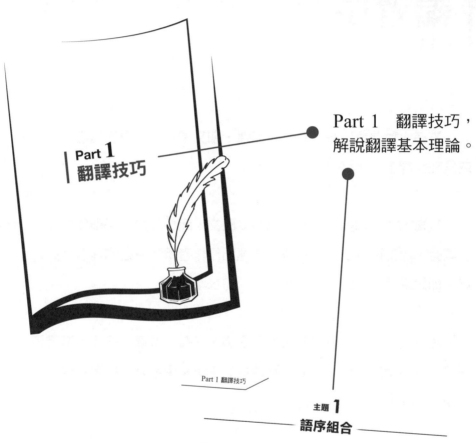

Part 1
翻譯技巧

Part 1　翻譯技巧，
解說翻譯基本理論。

主題 1
語序組合

英翻中

　　中文與英文本就是兩種截然不同的語言，雖然說語法順序上似乎大致上皆是主詞＋動詞＋受詞，但細究起來，還是有不少差異存在。當我們進行英翻中翻譯時，由於目標語言 - 中文，相對於來源語言 - 英文，是一種表意的象形文字，本質上不同於英文的拼音文字，它雖不需要在文法上有明顯的可條列出的並遵循的文法規則，但卻需在邏輯、情境、意涵上要能做出合理的呈現處理，是一種「意和」，並須依賴文境意義與邏輯關係來連結詞語與句子。

　　在進行英翻中時，中文語序在人、事、地、物等面向上，習慣從大範圍講到小範圍；先講整體，再講個體；由大的講到小的；從寬的先講，再講到窄的；先提遠的再講近的；以地址的呈現為例，就能發現明顯的不同，例如：

英中對照

Commercial ads are the most common advertisement, and they often seek to generate increased consumption of their products or services through "branding", which involves associating a product name or image with certain qualities in the minds of consumers. There are several categories of advertisement, such as product ads, recruiting ads, housing ads, magazine ads, tourism ads and event ads. The followings are some advertisement samples.

Part 2 主題範例，提供譯文英中對照，熟悉各領域的翻譯文章。

中文

商業廣告是最常見的廣告，讓產品名稱或是產品形象與消費者的心產生連結，以造成對產品或服務消費的增加。商業廣告有數種類別，如產品廣告、徵人廣告、房仲廣告、雜誌廣告、旅遊廣告、活動廣告，以下有幾個廣告樣本：

相關句型翻譯要點

相關句型翻譯要點，提點翻譯時要注意的重點！

1. 原　文 "There are several categories of advertisement, such as product ads, recruiting ads, housing ads, magazine ads, tourism ads, event ads." such as 通常翻作「如…」，後面常接對等的句子或是詞語。另有 etc. 的用法，常會被誤用來表示「…等等」，其實這種 such as 與 etc. 同時出現在同一句子的情況應避免，避開中文化英文之嫌，若已用了 such as 帶出了例子，較後面的文句中就不需要再使用 etc. 等等來增加贅字，西方人是不這麼使用英文的。

前輩指點

看看前輩的經驗談，避免多走冤枉路！

　　一般人可能對翻譯工作者有著「英文很好」或其某專業語文能力很好的概念。其實實際情況並非皆是如此，大部分翻譯工作者，雖普遍為專業語文相關科系學生，但也有不少譯者本身並非語文科班出身。筆者即是一例，並且也未正式研修過翻譯專業課程。專業的翻譯相關學位不見得是成為專業翻譯工作者的必要條件。

Contents

目次

Part 1 翻譯技巧

Part 2 主題範例

主題1 廣告

Part 1
翻譯技巧

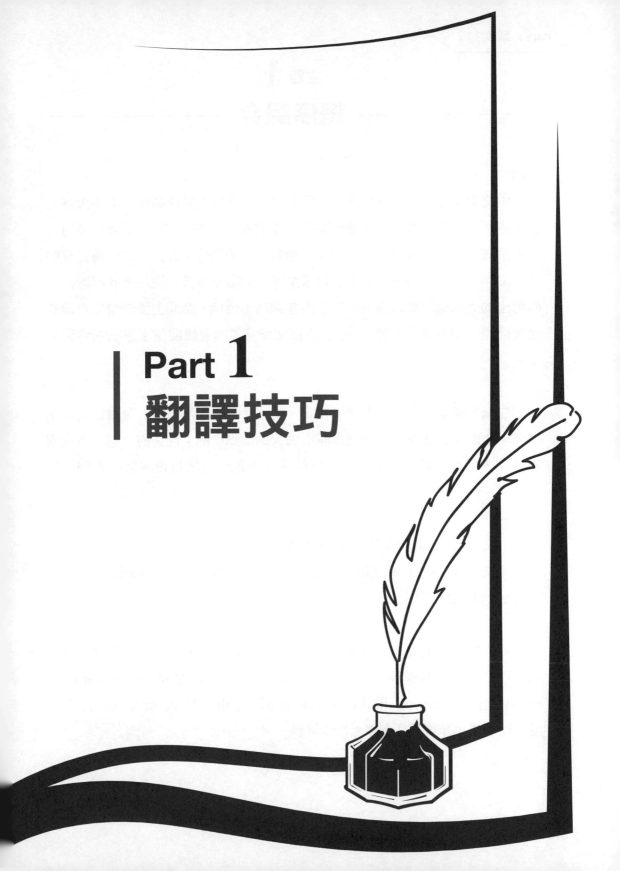

主題 1

語序組合

英翻中

　　中文與英文本就是兩種截然不同的語言，雖然說語法順序上似乎大致上皆是主詞＋動詞＋受詞，但細究起來，還是有不少差異存在。當我們進行英翻中翻譯時，由於目標語言 - 中文，相對於來源語言 - 英文，是一種表意的象形文字，本質上不同於英文的拼音文字，它雖不需要在文法上有明顯的可條列出的並遵循的文法規則，但卻需在邏輯、情境、意涵上要能做出合理的呈現處理，是一種「意和」，並須依賴文境意義與邏輯關係來連結詞語與句子。

　　在進行英翻中時，中文語序在人、事、地、物等面向上，習慣從大範圍講到小範圍；先講整體，再講個體；由大的講到小的；從寬的先講，再講到窄的；先提遠的再講近的；以地址的呈現為例，就能發現明顯的不同，例如：

中文地址 - 台北市光復南路 100 號
英文地址 -No.100, Guangfu S. Rd., Xinyi Dist., Taipei City 110, Taiwan（R.O.C.）

　　又以機關團體為例，一定按順序先從上大層級往下層較小單位呈現，如：行政院衛生署健保局，不像英文呈現方式為 the Bureau of National Health Insurance of the Department of Health, Executive Yuan. 是相反地從下層小單位漸往上層大單位呈現。

　　在時序上，中文要留意先發生的事情先說，後發生的事情後說。比方我們在描述某人一看到美食就會流口水，中文呈現上就不可能會寫成一流口水就知道是看到美食了，這在邏輯上就不合於「先發生的先說」的模式。由於在中文語序上有先後順序，相對地在陳述到因果關係時，也會依照先因後果的邏輯，先講原因再講結果，已知訊息在前、新知訊息在後，讓步在前、陳述在後，條件在前、結果在後，當進行英翻中時，在來源文章遇到 because, for, since, for 等表示因果的連接詞時，翻譯出來中文句子就要留意前述的先因後果及時間先後邏輯，才不會譯出怪文。

1

翻譯技巧

2

主題範例

中翻英

　　談到中翻英時，以上在範圍、時序、因果上需注意的邏輯及規則，英文就不一定需要像中文一樣的表現方式。在時序上，英文不一定需要依照先發生的先說，後發生的後說原則，它可以藉由一些介系詞、連接詞及動詞的時態等語法來表達時間順序，因此不用嚴守時間順序。相對的，延伸至因果面向上，英文中就沒有一定是「前」因「後」果的呈現方式。它也有可能先講完事情最後的結果後，才逆向回述導致此結果的原因。

　　從以下例文可看出其不同：

　　中文：《華爾街日報》出版者道瓊斯集團表示，因為廣告收入比預期少，第一季營收將遠低於分析師的估算。

　　英　文：Dow Jones & Co., publisher of The Wall Street Journal, said its first-quarter earnings will be sharply below analysts' expectations because of weaker-than-anticipated advertising revenue. （AP）（先講結果再帶出原因）

中譯成英文也可以以下呈現，強調的重點則不同，但講的還是同一件事。

Due to the weaker-than-anticipated advertising revenue, publisher of the Wall Street Journal, Dow Jones & Co., announced that its first-quarter earnings will be sharply below analysts' expectation.（先把原因說出來再講結果）

不管英譯中或中譯英，了解中英文語序上的差異是譯者應該下的基本功，將幫助譯者在翻譯時能靈活採用相對應的策略，譯出可達到翻譯目地的成品。

1 翻譯技巧

2 主題範例

主題 **2**

翻譯句法問題

我們知道，每個單字有時不只一個意思，因詞性的不同，有不同詞意，而當此單字於某個句子的一部分時，它的意思也會由於相對於句子的地位，而呈現不同的意涵，因此翻譯時，句法的瞭解及掌握，也就相對重要了。

就句子相對應於單詞的關係，歸納出有四大方向：

1. 句子會限制單詞：句子會提供情境，此情境限制了單詞產生過多的意思。如同樣是 pick up，在「she pick up her son」及「she picked up some Spanish in Spain」中就有不同的意思，一個是接載，一個則是學會，不同的句子給予了兩種不同情境，不同的情境自然地限制了單詞的字義。

2. 句子會影響單詞的正負面含意：如同樣的 challenging，在 "this is a challenging time" 中就比 "this is a challenge game" 還更有著負面想法，不同的句子脈絡，能把單詞意義導向正面，也同樣的可以導向負面。

3. 文章中其他句子也會影響單詞含意，字義線索常隱藏於上下文中。

4. 單詞的加總不等於句子：翻譯不是數學，翻譯過程也絕對不是如 1+1=2 一樣。如 what she said is far from impressive. 整個句子為「什麼、他說、是、遠離、印象深刻的」，加總起來也不見得是一句子。

　　了解了句子對應於語詞的關係後，以下整理了一些基本的翻譯句型用法，來幫助想進行翻譯的朋友運用。

增譯法、減譯法

　　增譯法是在翻譯時依據目標語的句法規範和修辭習慣，在譯文中增添來源語沒有的詞彙，使訊息的傳達更流暢貼切，通常增譯法增添的詞種類包括動詞、名詞、形容詞、副詞等，以增譯副詞為例，通常是在形容詞前增加副詞，像是「真」「很」等字來使語句通暢。如 The watch is expensive. 那支錶很貴。另外，英文以時態的方式呈現時間順序時，在譯成中文時則可以增加表示先後順序的時間副詞，如：mother took out some vegetables from the fridge, washed them, and cooked them. 媽媽從冰箱拿出一些蔬菜，先洗過後再拿去煮。

　　減譯法也可以說是省略法，是依據目標語的句法規範和修辭習慣，減少或省略來源語中某些詞彙，使譯文精煉簡潔。此處介紹了減譯虛主詞的用法，通常虛主詞是不需譯出的，如：It is easy to understand her lecture. 聽懂她的講課很容易。另外，分裂句中的 it 與 there 不須譯出。如：It is the man that saved the little girl.

詞類轉換

　　在翻譯的過程中，將來源語轉換為不同詞性目標語的翻譯技巧。如：The movie features dazzling special effects. 這部電影的特色是炫目的特效。原 feature 是動詞，在此轉換譯成名詞。

正反表達

　　即是正話反說、反話正說，運用正話反譯或反話正譯的方式，產出語法邏輯都通順的譯文。就是將原本正面表達的肯定句在譯文中以反面的否定方式來表達。原文否定句型譯成肯定句型，則是將原本正面表達的肯定句以文中以反面的否定方式來表達。

　　如：She walked out of the door without shoes.

　　反話反譯：她沒穿鞋就走出門。

　　反話正譯：她光著腳走出門。

　　這裡的 without shoe 可譯成「沒穿鞋子」，也可以用反話正譯，把它說成「光著腳，為中文習慣的表達方式。

順譯法、逆譯法

　　順譯就是依照原文字詞、片語或子句順序翻譯，不需改變原文形式結構，是種基本譯法。逆譯則是將原文的字詞、片語或子句順序顛倒過來 翻 譯。 如：She decided to listen to his advice and pulled herself together. 譯成「她決定聽取他的建議，好好振作。」

　　而以下例子，則是相反的逆譯法：

I went shopping with a friend from college yesterday.

我昨天跟大學時的朋友去逛街

被動語態

　　被動語態的翻譯方法有兩大類，一為「英文被動譯為中文被動」，通常這類多可分為「被」字句，「遭／受字句」及「使／把字句」例子如下：

Though he kept a very low profile, his secrets were still discovered.

雖然他行事非常低調，他的秘密還是被發現了。

The newly launched iPhone was warmly received by the market.
剛推出的 iPhone 受到市場廣大的歡迎

Peter was grounder by his father for getting into a fight at school.
彼得在學校與人打架，他父親把他禁足了。

　　另一類是「英文被動譯為中文主動」，有直接譯為主動語態的，像是 This ship was destined to Rotterdam. 這艘船預定開往鹿特丹。也有加入／不加入施事者的主動語態，例如：he is well known for his generosity. 大家都知道他的慷慨。(此處施事者即為大家)。另一種不加入施事者的主動語態，即是常看到的 it is believed…,it is said……, it is reported 等開頭的句子，我們常會譯成「據說…」、「聽說…」如：It is said that 2020 would bring about the end of the world. 據說 2020 年將是世界末日。

多句 - 合句、分句、重組

合句即是把來源語兩個以上的句子譯成目標語的一個句子，可以因此而精簡譯文。如 Connie owns a beautiful house. She is living her dream. 把原先兩句的譯文「康尼擁有一棟美房。她實現了她夢想」合成一句譯為「康尼實現了擁有美房的夢想」。

分句則相反地把單一英文簡單句譯成兩個以上的中文句子，常將一些單詞如形容詞、名詞等拆離後譯成中文短句。如以下例句：

She wears long and silky shiny hair.

原：她有一頭又長又柔又亮的頭髮。

經拆離後，譯成：她一頭長髮，又柔又亮。

重組即是脫離英文原文的句式結構和訊息排序，遵循中文的行文敘事習慣重新改寫成譯文，通常處理複雜的長句。此法可以擺脫原文語法句型限制，專注在如何使譯文更加自然流暢。通常須將原文的長句結構先分析清楚，並且將各訊息間的邏輯關係理解透徹，整個分成數個可能的翻譯單位，之後再按照中文的表達習慣，重新組合這些單位而成為譯文。

以下文例可供為參考：

原文

Nothing inspired us more as we watched the breathtaking performance of the gymnasts than the final jump of the Chinese player that put the Chinese boys on the champion stand.

譯作

當我們在看體操選手們驚心動魄的表演時，沒有什麼能比那中國選手的最後一跳更振奮人心了，這一跳使得中國男孩們登上了冠軍台。

事實上，應該翻譯了一陣子後，絕大部分的情況就幾乎都是在做重組功夫。它幾乎就是各種翻譯方法的整合了。

主題 **3**
超翻漏翻

在進行翻譯時，有時候會有超翻與漏翻的情形發生。

超翻就是指「超額翻譯」（overtranslation），翻出來的譯文超出了原文，多增加了原文沒有的東西。而漏翻則是「欠額翻譯」（undertranslation），就是譯文不及原文，省略掉原文中有提到的某些東西。其實翻譯時這兩種情況都是無可避免的。而不管是超翻或是漏翻，這兩種情況都算是部分翻譯，而不是全文翻譯。

像甜甜圈 doughnut 一詞，原意其實只是麵團，並沒有描述口味「甜甜」的意思，但我們翻成「甜甜圈」，這就是某種程度上的超翻。另外，把 "I wear on my glasses and continue the book reading" 翻成「我戴上了眼鏡並且繼續讀那本書」也是翻譯過多，其實只需要翻成「我戴上眼鏡看書」就可以了。有時，礙於語言結構、文化內涵或是民族色彩的差別，免不了需要補充一些額外的，才能完整的傳遞原先來源語言的真實涵義，但請切實注意這樣隨意的加油添醋、渲染等譯法，最大底限應該是不能無中生有的加上很多的額外事物。如英文句子 "The Secretary was on his way to the Middle East again." 譯成「國務卿不顧勞累，風塵僕僕地展開他的中東之行。」句子當中的「不顧勞累、風塵僕僕」等根本在原來的來源句子中並沒出現，應該刪除。

漏翻，也就是「欠額翻譯」（undertranslation），指的是翻的不夠，會有少掉沒有表達到的部分，如：使用 "my cousin" 表示「我表弟」，而不是使用 "my male cousin on my mother's side" 來表示「我表弟」。merry-go-round 旋轉木馬就沒將含有快樂涵義的 merry 譯出，也算是一種漏翻。例如：This is some war. 若只譯成「這是一場戰爭」，那就漏掉了原文真義了。在此其實應該翻作「這真是一場大戰」，完整意思才能表達到位。而以下句子 "The statesmen are used to flying a kite before an election campaign." 若只翻成「在選舉前政治家們習慣放風箏」，也算是遺漏了本句真正的背後意涵了，fly a kite 確實是指放風箏沒錯，但在這裡，其實它的真實意義是「試探大眾及輿論反應」，最好還是改譯為「在大選前政治家們習慣於試探一下公眾及輿論的反應。」

「超翻」與「漏翻」其實在翻譯中是不可避免的現象，因為超翻漏翻的情況，主要來自於語言與文化的差異，這差異相對於其他變數，其實是相對固定的，因此相對應的其他變數，像是譯者本身的翻譯技巧與方式，就成了造成超額或是欠額的主要變數了，光是同一譯者在不同時期對同一來源文就已經可能有不同的超翻和漏翻了，若是不同譯者，差異將更大，可以說超翻和漏翻，絕大部還是取決於譯者本身。

1

翻譯技巧

2

主題範例

主題 **4**

正式文件

一般人在日常生活中，常會因工作、學習或其他原因，而需以書面或文件與不同的個體、機關單位（含國家機關、企業、社會團體等）進行文字書面上的溝通、交流、傳遞訊息以達成某目的或處理某具體事務。由於此類型文件通常涉有效力，具有實用性質，又因對應個體常為機關團體，是眾人之事，相對於其他只是偏重較私密個人的表情抒懷抒情文體，或是紀錄事實的記敘文體，顯得相對正式，我們歸類此類文件為正式文件，大致上就如同於傳統中文文體分類中的「應用文」，包含了多種不同形式。

對應於機關單位時，通常有：公文、報告、計畫、章程、法律文件（筆錄、鑑定書、起訴書、調解書、判決書…等）多種不同形式及使用目的等文件。而當對企業或其他團體進行溝通時，最常見到的正式文件不外乎商業合約、財務報告、公開說明書、招投標書、保證書、說明書、市調報告等等。此外，再更小範圍一點的層級，也就是個體本身或家戶，會使用到的正式文件，不外乎為各式證件，如身分證、學生證、良民證、戶口名簿、學歷證件、駕照等。

針對以上各種不同的正式文件，不管是中翻英或是英翻中，其實都有固定約定俗成而來或是有具體規格的格式，除了文件中的特定專有名詞需使用固定的用字外，文件格式亦是另一需要特別注意的重點。若就公文翻譯而言，又因其譯出文與來源文所發揮出的作用與所具效力（含法律效力）相同，產生約束、命令的作用，譯者最好要能熟悉政府各部門運作詳情，才能確保譯出文的正確性與執行力。

公文

以公文為例，機關單位名稱為固定用字，可運用相關翻譯資源查詢到專用字來使用，另有一些公文中常用的固定句子，摘錄部分供參考：

- ××××年××月××日發佈（例如：2015 年 10 月 18 日發佈）

  英文翻譯：Issued on M D, Y（Issued on Oct. 18, 2015）

- ××××年××月××日實施（例如：2015 年 6 月 18 日實施）

  英文翻譯：Implemented on M D, Y（Implemented on June 18, 2015）

- 施行日期

  英文翻譯：Implementation date

- 現批准 ××× 為國家標準，標準編號為 ×××

  英文翻譯：××× has been approved as a national standard with a serial number of ×××

- ××× 為強制性條文，必須嚴格執行

  英文翻譯：××× are compulsory provisions and must be enforced strictly

- 原 ××× 同時廢止

  英文翻譯：××× shall be abolished simultaneously

- 本標準（規範）由教育局負責管理和對強制性條文的解釋

  英文翻譯：Education Bureau is in charge of the administration of this standard（code）and the explanation of the compulsory provisions

- 由 ××× 負責具體技術內容的解釋

  英文翻譯：××× is responsible for the explanation of specific technical contents

- 繼續有效

  英文翻譯：be valid as usual

- 備案

  英文翻譯：Put on records

- 前言

  英文翻譯：Foreword

- 本規範以黑體字標誌的條文為強制性條文，必須嚴格執行

  英文翻譯：The provision (s) printed in bold type is (are) compulsory one (ones) and must be enforced strictly.

- 請各單位在執行本標準過程中，總結經驗，積累資料，隨時將相關意見及建議寄交 ×××

  英文翻譯：All relevant organizations are kindly requested to sum up and accumulate experiences in actual practices during the process of implementing this code. The relevant opinions and advice, whenever necessary, can be posted or passed on to ×××

1

翻譯技巧

2

主題範例

商業合約

商業合約是另一經常使用到的正式文件，由於它也具有法律效力特質，在進行翻譯時，詞語需用公文詞語，特別是考量使用英文慣用的語副詞，如此方能使譯文達成結構嚴謹、邏輯嚴密與言簡意賅。以下摘錄一些商業合約常用的語副詞供參考：

從此以後、今後：hereafter	對於那個：whereto
此後、以後：thereafter	在上文：hereinabove, hereinbefore
在其上：thereonthereupon	在下文：hereinafter, hereinbelow
在其下：thereunder	在上文中、在上一部分中：thereinbefore
對於這個：hereto	在下文中、在下一部分中：thereinafter

合約翻譯成英文時，除副詞外，一些介詞的使用也須謹慎，以下為幾個須留意的用法：

- 遵守：comply with 與 abide by
  當主語是「非人」時，翻譯「遵守」須用 comply with；當主語是「人」時，則用 abide by。
  例：雙方都應遵守／雙方的一切活動都應遵守合約規定。
  All the activities of both parties shall comply with the contractual stipulations / Both parties shall abide by

- 運來／運走：ex 與 per

  ex 與 per 為源自拉丁語的介詞，有不同含意，翻譯由某輪船「運來」的貨物時用 ex，由某輪船「運走」的貨物用 per，而由某輪船「承運」用 by。

- 多少天之後：in 與 after

  當翻譯「多少天之後」的確切某天時，必須用介詞 in，不能用 after。而介詞 after 指的則是「多少天之後」的不確切的任何一天。

  例：該貨於 11 月 10 日由「維多利亞」輪運出，41 天後抵達鹿特丹港。The good shall be shipped per M.V. "Victoria" on November 10 and are due to arrive at Rottedaml in 140 days. (M.V. = motor vessel)

- ……之後，就……：on/upon 與 after

  當翻譯「……到後，就……」時，需用介詞 on/upon，而不用 after，因為 after 表示「之後」的時間不明確。

  例：發票貨值須貨到付給。The invoice value is to be paid on/upon arrival of the goods.

- ……之前：by 與 before

當翻譯終止時間時，比如「在某月某日之前」，如果包括所寫日期時，就用介詞 by；如果不包括所寫日期，即指到所寫日期的前一天為止，就要用介詞 before。

例：賣方須在 9 月 8 日前將貨交給買方。

The vendor shall deliver the goods to the vendee by Sep.8.（或：before Sep. 9，說明含 9 月 8 日在內。如果不含 9 月 8 日，就譯為 by Sep.7 或者 before Sep. 8。）

　　商業合約對於細目，如：金錢、時間、數量等要更特別注意並為避免出錯，通常在翻譯時，常常使用一些有限定作用的結構來界定細目所指定的確切範圍，如限定責任、時間、金額等。限定責任時使用 and/or、by and between；限定時間時，常用雙介詞，如 no later than 或 include 的相應形式 (inclusive, included, including) 等來限定含當日在內的時間。金額方面，為避免金額數量的差漏、偽造或塗改，翻譯時需特別注意以下措施：大寫文字重複金額，翻譯金額須在小寫之後，在括弧內用大寫文字重複該金額，即使原文合約中沒有大寫，翻譯時也有必要加上大寫。在大寫文字前加上 "SAY"，意為「大寫」；在最後加上 "ONLY"，意思為 "整"。必須注意：小寫與大寫的金額數量要一致。另外還需注意正確使用貨幣符號，如 "$" 既可代表「美元」，又可代表其他某些地方的貨幣；而 "£" 不僅代表「英鎊」，又可代表其他某些地方的貨幣。還要特別注意金額中是小數點 (.)，還是分節號 (,)，這兩個符號極易引起筆誤，稍有疏忽，後果將不堪設想。

　　另外一種常需要翻譯的正式文件為各式證件，如戶籍謄本、出生證明、結婚證書、學歷證明、成績單、兵役證明、良民證、在職／服務證明、公司執照、營利事業登記證、股東變更登記等，通常除了內容須確認與原文無誤外，此類文件一般要求須經過公證，才會予以承認，此點則需特別注意。

1

翻譯技巧

2

主題範例

主題 **5**
非正式文件

　　非正式文件有別於前面篇章的「正式文件」，相對上不具有法律效力、公眾事務趨向等特性，形式上更顯多樣，內容更複雜，涵蓋範圍也更寬廣，從文學作品（含小說、散文、詩、劇本）、科技文件、歌曲、廣告等，至新聞報刊、演講、論文，運用相當廣泛。在此我們大致以文學性非正式文件與非文學性非正式文件來略述一下此類文件的翻譯。

　　文學可說是一種語言的藝術，用來反映現實、抒發情感與表達思想，為感性導向，包含了小說、散文、詩歌、戲劇等文字形式。進行文學翻譯時，主要須注重美學考量，不僅注重字對字、詞對詞的翻譯，更不能忽略文化差異，否則將會導致譯文在語意、美感、風格上的流失。

文學性

　　以翻譯英語小說為例，通常小說反映的是廣闊社會現實，譯者最好對英語民族與國家的社會文化知識等，有一定程度的涉獵，此將增進對原著的正確理解。同時譯者也需對於譯出的目地語言如中文，有高等程度的運用能力，造句遣詞上才得以避免過於西化的句型出現，確保行文流暢。另一項特別注意的重點是想像力與聯想能力，想像力是小說家的重要稟賦，譯者應在此面向上，盡最大限度地接近原作家。

散文的翻譯，與小說的翻譯類似，首重準確把握原文的內容及風格。早期英文散文多為說明或勸諭文字，風格簡潔樸實，有口語化傾向，如十七世紀培根的散文就多用排比並列的句型呈現，至十九世紀整體文學界受浪漫主義思潮影響，風格轉為典雅華麗，作家直抒所想，運用靈活文句、新穎語言，使作品極富強烈感染力，生動比喻、強烈節奏及飛揚的文采即為當時的散文時代特色。譯者若能了解其時代風格背景的話，有助於譯出符合真實情況的作品。

詩可說是翻譯工作中最難翻譯的文體了，不管是中譯英或是英譯中，幾乎是不可能準確翻譯的，因為詩歌通常涉及形式、音韻，特別是格律詩，要能形式與音韻兼具，難度相當高。而詩的翻譯，可分意、形、神三層次來看，首重意求真、形求相似、神求生動活化。求真其實與翻譯任何其他文體時都一樣，是基本要求，型態上，某些譯者會把英文詩依中文詩五言、七言等格式譯出，搭配音韻或不搭配音韻的斟酌後譯出作品，搭配音韻者，會以頓代步，即運用語音自然的抑揚頓挫來翻譯。另有部分譯者在翻譯英語格律詩時，會放棄在音韻上搭配，轉而採取自由體的格式，畢竟有時硬要搭配音韻，反而束縛了真實意境的表達。以下摘錄一例比較供參考：

1 翻譯技巧

2 主題範例

The curfew tolls the knell of parting day,

The lowing herd wind slowly o'er the lea,

The plowman homeward plods his weary way,

And leaves the world to darkness and to me.

譯文一：

晚鐘響起來一陣陣給白晝報喪

牛群在草原上迂迴，吼聲起落

耕地人累了，回家腳步踉蹌

把整個世界給了黃昏與我

譯文二：

晚鐘殷殷響，夕陽已西沉

群牛呼叫歸，迂迴走草徑

農人荷鋤犁，倦倦回家門

唯我立曠野，獨自對黃昏

非文學性

　　非文學性的非正式文件，種類相當多，範圍也相當廣泛，如科技文件、廣告、新聞報刊、演講、論文…等，光新聞文件中，就有新聞報導、新聞特寫、分析評論等體裁。新聞報導多半採用延伸的簡單句，多以直接或間接引語開展句子，大多數以主動語態達到敘事的客觀與便利，同時，使用現在式，使讀者產生一種「某事正在發生」的印象，標題亦常使用省略句。結構上，新聞文件多半有標題、導言、正文、結語，並兼有倒金字塔層次結構，譯者須對這些特性有基礎認知，進行翻譯時，做到以下：

■ 準確理解一些常用詞語在新聞英語中的特定含意。

■ 要使譯文文體風格與原文相適應。

■ 妥善處理新聞中的新詞或新造字詞。新詞即為字典中查不到的詞，遇到此類詞時，可在詞形上加以辨析找出字根或字首等，幫助理解詞意，也可從上下文中，即該詞與其他詞的搭配、組合中尋找線索，判斷其可能的意義。

■ 行文力求簡明。即不參雜情緒因素，語言務求平實，勿浮華誇張，在名詞前加修飾語時要慎重。

1

翻譯技巧

2

主題範例

- 釐清原文中的一些特殊語法現象，譯文時不要被某些動詞語態所惑。如 Large Chinese trade delegation to visit US in Novemeber., 中間其實省略了 to 之前的 is，而像 2 workmen injured in electrical accident 則其實真正原意為 2 workmen are injured...

- 標題翻譯要盡量與原文依樣簡短，要能使譯文向原文一樣傳神達意。如：four killed and five hurt in a house fire 房屋起火四死五傷；Soccer kicks off with violence 足球開賽拳打腳踢

　　很多非文學類文本的翻譯工作，包括軟體手冊和其他商業及專業文本，注重的是意義的傳達，以能通順傳意為主要要求。在全球化的潮流下，不但有越來越多的國際組織，同時企業的經營也越來越以全球觀點出發，其實這也帶動了國際化與本地化產業的興起。

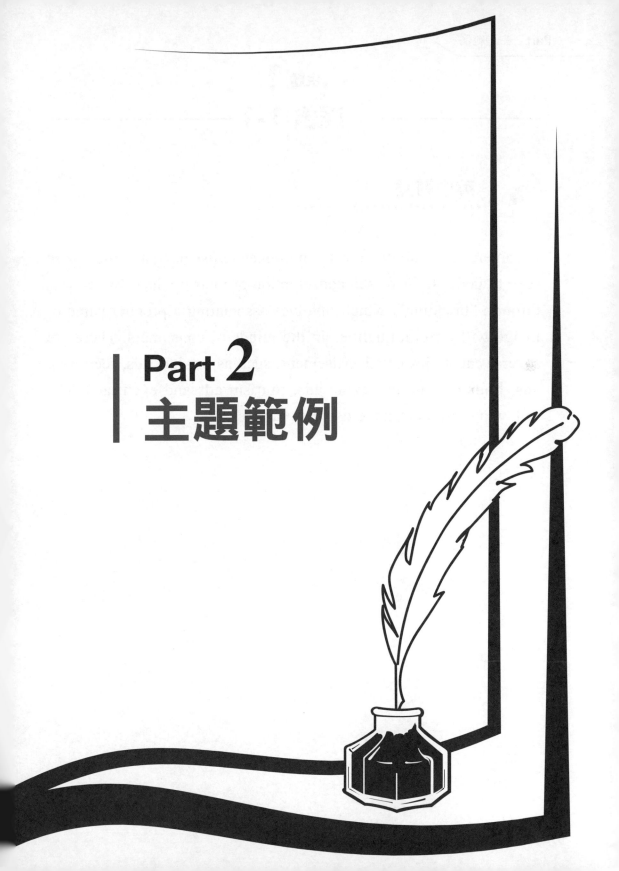

Part 2
主題範例

主題 **1**
廣告 1-1

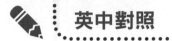

英中對照

Commercial ads are the most common advertisement, and they often seek to generate increased consumption of their products or services through "branding", which involves associating a product name or image with certain qualities in the minds of consumers. There are several categories of advertisement, such as product ads, recruiting ads, housing ads, magazine ads, tourism ads and event ads. The followings are some advertisement samples.

Product ads:

PAMELA

THE WINTER COLLECTION

This winter, Pamela will lead you on a journey to a world frozen in time filled with crystalized silhouettes; glittering snowflakes, snow-dusted flowers and twinkling stars.

BE INSPIRED

Pamela is going to make your jewelry not just jewelry. With ruby red facets, crystalized blues, and glittering snowflakes, you are able to find your perfect winter style.

RINGS start from USD 55.00

NECKLACES start from USD70.00

EARINGS start from USD45.00

BRACELETS start from USD60.00

Housing ads:

151-155 Stanton Road, Smithfield QLD 4878–High $800,000s

6 bedrooms

3 bathrooms

2 cars parking spaces

Architecturally designed impressive hideaway house-property!!

This tranquil home is sure to impress! Nestled in the tree tops of the exclusive Stanton Road, set on 1.38 hectares with spectacular views of the Northern beaches. This stunning home is a must see and is perfect for someone looking for space, privacy and views in a peaceful rainforest setting, and it is conveniently located close to local amenities including Smithfield shopping center and local schools.

Features include:

- Six large bedrooms
- Two bathrooms including ensuite to master bedroom
- Stunning high ceilings throughout
- Upstairs with large modern kitchen, large living area and veranda amongst the treetops
- Separate self-contained living downstairs, also with its own veranda
- Sweeping driveway with automatic gate
- Has its very own rock pool

Owner sale, please contact Jason 0488597345

Recruiting ads:

EXCELLENT JOB OPPORTUNITIES

For a reputed Sugar Millers in the TTA province

GM administrator for sugar millers

Qualification: Graduate

Accountant

Qualification: MBA, ACA

Purchaser

Qualification: Minimum intermediate degree

Computer data processor

Qualification: Graduate

Note

Application along with attested copies of Degree, Certificate, Testimonies, two passport size photographs may be sent to **BOX NO.264, Market City, NSW 2086.**

Apply within 15 days of this advertisement

Tourism ads:

GRTEAT BARRIER REEF ADVENTURES

Day includes

- Relaxed 9:30am departure from Reef Fleet Terminal with 4 hours at the reef
- Snorkeling enclosure with rest and view stations
- Free glass bottom boat & semi-submersible tours
- Fully enclosed kids pool
- Marine life touch tank
- Fish feeding presentation
- Tropical buffet lunch with seafood
- Optional diving, Snorkel tours, Seawalker platform dive & Helicopter scenic flights

Depart Cairns Wharf $199 per adult (children and family prices on request.)

SUN Q Reef Cruises

Free call 1800 123 123

中文

商業廣告是最常見的廣告，讓產品名稱或是產品形象與消費者的心產生連結，以造成對產品或服務消費的增加。商業廣告有數種類別，如產品廣告、徵人廣告、房仲廣告、雜誌廣告、旅遊廣告、活動廣告，以下有幾個廣告樣本：

產品廣告：

潘蜜拉

冬季系列

今年冬天，潘蜜拉將領你進入一個充滿結晶輪廓、光彩奪目雪花、覆雪花朵與閃亮星辰的冰凍世界旅程。

啟發

潘蜜拉使你的珠寶不只是珠寶而已，紅寶石紅琢面、水晶藍及光亮雪花等，讓你有無限的選擇，找到你的完美冬日風格。

戒指 55 元起
項鍊 70 元起
耳環 45 元起
手環 60 元起

房仲廣告：

151-155 Stanton Road, Smithfield QLD 4878 最高 $800,000 元

六房
三衛浴
雙車庫

隱匿性極高之設計房產物件！

此寧靜的家絕對讓你印象深刻，獨家坐落於 Stanton Road 樹間，占地 1.38 公頃，擁有北部海灘的壯闊視野。如此雨林中的絕色美房為尋求空間、隱蔽型及好視野的買房人士必看物件，相當方便的鄰近當地設施如 Smithfield 購物中心及學校。

特色：

六大房

兩套主臥室獨立衛浴

絕色高天花板貫穿

大現代化廚房位於樓上，大起居空間，樹間走廊

樓下分離的自給自足起居空間並含走廊

全面自動門車道

自家岩石水池

屋主自售，請聯絡 Jason 0488597345

徵人廣告：

絕佳工作機會

TTA 省某磨糖廠

總經理

資格：大學畢業

會計

資格：MBA 或 ACA 學位

採購

資格：中等學位以上

電腦資料處理員

資格：大學畢業

注意事項

應徵者請將學歷證明、證書、推薦信及兩張護照大小照片寄至 **BOX NO.264, Market City, NSW 2086.**

請在此廣告 15 天內應徵

旅遊廣告：

大堡礁探險

行程包含

- 放鬆地早晨 9:30 從凱恩斯遊船碼頭出發，四小時待在礁岩上
- 有休息及觀景平台的範圍浮潛
- 免費玻璃底船及半潛水行程
- 全圈遊小孩泳池
- 海洋生物觸摸池
- 餵魚展演
- 熱帶海鮮自助式午餐
- 選擇性潛水、浮潛行程，海底漫步平台潛水與直升機觀景

凱恩斯碼頭出發 每人 $199 元起（孩童及家庭票價格另洽）

SUN Q 堡礁郵輪

免費電話 1800 123 123

單字片語解釋

- associate... with... 把…和…連繫在一起
  They associate turkey with Thanksgiving.
  他們把火雞和感恩節聯繫在一起。

- crystalized　v.　結晶、使結晶
  Salt is crystalized from seawater.
  鹽是從海水中結晶的。

- silhouettes　n.　輪廓
  Mary describes lover's face in silhouettes.
  Mary 描述了愛人的臉部輪廓。

- inspire　v.　啟示、使生靈感
  The shape of star inspires his creative artwork.
  他的創意藝術作品乃是由星星的形狀得到靈感而來。

- nestle　v.　舒適地安頓下來、安臥
  The dog nestled in the small house.
  那隻狗安臥在小屋裡。

- snorkel　n.　浮潛
  They went snorkeling along the Great Barrier Reef.
  他們沿著大堡礁浮潛。

相關句型翻譯要點

1. 原　文 "There are several categories of advertisement, such as product ads, recruiting ads, housing ads, magazine ads, tourism ads, event ads." such as 通常翻作「如…」，後面常接對等的句子或是詞語。另有 etc. 的用法，常會被誤用來表示「…等等」，其實這種 such as 與 etc. 同時出現在同一句子的情況應避免，避開中文化英文之嫌，若已用了 such as 帶出了例子，較後面的文句中就不需要再使用 etc. 等等來增加贅字，西方人是不這麼使用英文的。

2. 廣告的翻譯，除了實際價錢或涉及資訊的文字照翻之外，其餘的文案部分其實比較注重形容詞的修飾，以能達到增強閱聽人心理連結的功用，好藉此增加其購買欲望，讓此廣告發揮實際作用。強調心理層面的訴求，就比較不需要固守逐字照翻的原則，以意境為主，以最能鼓動消費者並產生共鳴的方向譯作為妥。制式文法與文章結構不是主要重點。

前輩指點

　　一般人可能對翻譯工作者有著「英文很好」或其某專業語文能力很好的概念。其實實際情況並非皆是如此，大部分翻譯工作者，雖普遍為專業語文相關科系學生，但也有不少譯者本身並非語文科班出身。筆者即是一例，並且也未正式研修過翻譯專業課程。專業的翻譯相關學位不見得是成為專業翻譯工作者的必要條件。

　　筆者本人並非外國語文相關科系學生，畢業踏入社會後其實從事的工作也並翻譯相關工作，不過倒是在一開始踏入職場之初從事過編輯工作，算也是與翻譯相同性質的工作。之所以會踏入翻譯工作領域，也算是機緣巧合，當時人在國外留學，因耳聞翻譯證照或是擁有專業翻譯學歷的留學生因技術為當地所需，申請技術移民成功的機率很大，因此便趁課程結束簽證未到期前針對此一證照的考試做準備，算是排遣一下無所事事的時間，就這麼進入了翻譯領域，其實這麼走一遭下來，我會說翻譯工作者並不見得英文或是某一外語要非常非常好，但他的本身語文基底絕對要到達一定水準，能運用得宜，才能做好翻譯工作。

主題 1
廣告 1-2

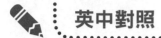 英中對照

Nowadays, it has become easier than before for entrepreneurs to start businesses due to the rapid development of the Internet. Many small businesses even adopt virtual shops as their major selling channel without opening physical shops. Through advertising marketing strategies that are reliant on storytelling, some famous online shops are even extendeding to physical shops, where consumers are lining up.

Here is a good example of storytelling. This brand set up a selling channel on the Internet in the beginning, and then expended to a physical shop later on. The following is the story.

ELATE created by chance from a father's love

In the hot summer of 1999, a father who is good at cooking felt sorry for his youngest daughter who was engaged in the preparation for the university entrance exam. His daughter was getting emaciated because of a lack of appetite and the father did not know how to express his care. He then attentively made juicy milk puddings with a rich milky aroma and nutrition to replace his daughter's daily diet. This delicious pudding made with benevolence not only revealed her father's care and support for the daughter, but also accidently built a reputation with friends and relatives. The pudding became the most satisfying of Mr. Feng's dessert.

The brand name, ELATE is translated from the pronunciation of satisfied in Chinese (DE YI), and this HOME MADE brand was created by chance. The original spirit of the product is faithfully reproduced in each dessert as if it were made for the family.

ELETE pudding sustains its sincereness by selling a trust-worthy product with a 100% fresh promise in addition to positive entrepreneurship from the start. It has earned most recognition from the public.

中文

　　近年來由於網路發達，開店創業變得較於以往容易，很多小型企業在開業之初甚至採取無實體店面的模式，以網路為主要行銷管道，並靠著「說故事」的廣告行銷手法，造就不少名店，一些甚至擴展至實體店面，成為排隊名店。

　　分享一個故事說得不錯的例子，此品牌最先發展之初也是先在網路販售，後來才有實體店面。故事是這樣的：

依蕾特意外誕生　源自一位父親的愛心

　　1999 年炎熱的夏天，看著準備大學聯考日夜苦讀身心疲憊的小女兒，因為沒有食慾而日漸消瘦，平日善廚的父親覺得十分心疼而又不知如何表達關切之情，於是著手細心地調理出乳香濃郁、富水感而又兼具營養的鮮奶布丁，來替代女兒每日的餐點，而這可口又充滿愛心的布丁不但表達了對女兒的支持與關心，也意外地受到眾多親友的口碑好評，成為方爸爸的「最得意」甜點作品。

　　品牌名 ELATE 音譯為得意的意思，也意外催生了依蕾特這個自製品牌，產品原創精神就是堅持以作給家人吃的誠摯心意，來製作每一個令人感動的甜點。

　　依蕾特布丁奶酪除了品牌建立之初鮮明而有正能量的誠摯心意外，更秉著誠懇心意，堅持賣一份讓人安心享用、100% 新鮮的產品，獲得了廣大消費者的肯定。

　　（以上摘自網站上品牌故事原文）

單字片語解釋

- entrepreneur　*n.*　創業家、企業家
  Jason has become an entrepreneur working for himself.
  傑森已經成為為自己工作的創業家。

- virtual　*adj.*　虛擬的
  Virtual shop saves a lot of operation cost.
  虛擬商店節省很多營運成本。

- emaciated　*adj.*　消瘦的、憔悴的
  It is rare to see the emaciated children on the street in this country.
  很難在這國家的街道上看到消瘦的孩童。

- appetite　*n.*　胃口、食慾
  Jane does not have much appetite because of the illness.
  珍因為生病而不太有胃口。

- benevolence　*n.*　善意、慈悲、善行
  She smiles to me with benevolence.
  她朝我釋放善意微笑。

- earn recognition 得到肯定
  Jack earns the recognition from the management based on his excellent work performance.
  傑克的傑出工作表現得到管理階層的認可。

🔍 相關句型翻譯要點

1. 原中文邏輯大多以直述方式鋪陳，但譯作英文時，必須依時態來選用適當文法完成句子。原中文「近年來由於網路發達，開店創業變得較於以往容易，很多小型企業在一開業之初甚至採取無實體店面的模式…」描述的是一種現象，所以就全部以「現在式」譯出，成 Nowadays, it has become easier than before for entrepreneurs to start businesses due to the rapid development of the Internet. Many small businesses even adopt virtual shops as their major selling channel without opening physical shops.

2. 第二段述說的產品品牌故事實例，因為時間背景為 1999 年夏天，已是過去發生的事情，所以譯成英文時，使用過去式，如 a father who is good at cooking felt sorry for his youngest daughter who was engaged in the preparation for the university entrance exam. His daughter was getting emaciated because of a lack of appetite and the father did not know how to express his care. He then attentively made juicy milk puddings with a rich milky aroma and nutrition to replace his daughter's daily diet.

⭐ 前輩指點

　　翻譯新手一般比較難在一開始時就接到翻譯書籍的案子，因為目前在台灣主流語文（英、日、法語等）市場，均已有經驗豐富的專業資深翻譯，已能足夠包辦現有書籍翻譯市場，案子就不一定會釋出到一般兼職翻譯人員，因此建議先以小規模的翻譯機會起頭會比較容易些。可以透過翻譯公司或翻譯社，先翻譯文件，例如合約、廣告、商業信件等等，隨時都有需求，它們通常內容不長，講究的是清楚明白、言簡意賅，是入門練習的好機會。

　　若真有心要成為專職翻譯工作者，朝翻譯書籍的目標邁進，其實也可在入行之際開始多做練習，累積並培養實力。可自發性的翻譯佳文小品，發表於各式媒體，如網路、報紙、雜誌等，也可以自己經營部落格，反應若是正向的，相信行之日久後，會有人自動找上門來請你翻譯的。

主題 1
——— 廣告 1-3 ———

英中對照

There are different types of advertising, and celebrity branding is one of them. A celebrity becomes a brand ambassador and uses his or her status in society to promote or endorse a product, service or charity. It can be taken in several different forms, from the appearance of a celebrity in advertisements for a product, service or charity, to a celebrity attending PR events, creating his or her own line of products or services, or using his or her name as a brand.

Clothing and fragrances are the most popular product lines that build the brand by celebrity branding. Singers, models, and film stars may have licensed products bear their names. For instance, the use of a celebrity or a sports professional can have an influence on a brand such as Nike and Adidas. For example, Nike launched a series of Air Jordan for basketball star Michael Jordan and gained marketing success in 1984.

Some celebrities have distinct voices that are recognizable even when faces are not visible on a screen; therefore, they may also provide voice-overs for advertising. For example, the super model Lin Chi-ling and the famous TV host Li Jing in Taiwan have many ads with voice-overs only.

Celebrity branding is a global phenomenon. Since celebrities enjoy reputation, attractiveness and public recognition, and most of them are associated with a remarkable life; consequently, the public may treat them as virtual demigods in some countries such as India. There is also a correlation between brand endorsements and celebrity branding. For example, the Indian actor Sharukh khan who starred in *My Name Is Khan* has just endorsed various products because of his prestige.

In some cases, celebrity endorsement can bring negative effects rather than enhancement for the product due to mistaken appeal. The commercial ad that Nicole Kidman endorsed for the United Arab Emirates' Etihad Airways has brought critics from different parties. There is a conflict between the brand image and celebrity recognition. The endorsement did not go well.

中文

廣告有很多種，名人品牌建立是其中一種，名人變成品牌大使並使用他的社經地位來促銷或代言產品、服務或是慈善活動。名人品牌活動可用數種不同形式進行，從名人在產品、服務或慈善廣告中露臉，到名人參加公關活動、創建其個人產品線，或是使用名人名字做為品牌。

最流行運用名人品牌活動的產品線為服飾與香水產品。一些歌手、模特兒、電影明星，至少會有一項掛著他／她名字的授權商品或服務。啟用名人或專業運動員來做品牌活動對品牌有很大的影響，例如：耐吉 NIKE 在 1984 年時發表了籃球運動明星麥可喬登代言的 Air Jordan 系列，後來在行銷上獲得大成功。

一些名人的聲音辨識度高，即使他的臉不出現在螢幕上都能被認得，因此名人也提供廣告旁白來代言，如台灣名模林志玲及電視主持人利菁，她們就有為數不少的廣告旁白作品。

名人品牌活動是全球現象。名人享有聲譽、吸引力及大眾認可，他們大部份過著非凡的生活，因此在一些國家，如印度，更被視為半人半神崇拜著。而成功的名人品牌活動與品牌代言間亦有關聯性，如印度片 *My name is Khan* 中的知名男星 Sharukh khan 就因為他的聲望而代言了相當多產品。

有時候名人代言也可能因訴求被誤解而有反效果，而沒能對產品有助益。妮可基嫚為阿提哈德航空拍的廣告就惹來不同團體的批評。產品形象與大眾對名人本身的身分識別有矛盾之處，使得此代言效果並不好。

單字片語解釋

- celebrity　*n.*　名人
  Dr. Lin is a national celebrity.
  林醫師是全國聞名的人

- ambassador　*n.*　大使、代表
  He was appointed the ambassador of France.
  他被任命為駐法國大使。

- appearance　*n.*　外貌、外表
  The appearance of the old house completely changed.
  那所舊房子的外觀全變了。

- phenomenon　*n.*　現象
  Glaciers are interesting natural phenomena.
  冰河是有趣的自然現象

- demigod　*n.*　半人半神、受崇拜的人
  Can men be turned to a demigod?
  人可以變成神嗎？

- endorsement　*n.*　背書、支持、認可
  The package was regarded as an endorsement of the government's
  reform program.
  整個配套被視為政府改革計畫的背書。

🔍 相關句型翻譯要點

1. 原文 "It can be taken in several different forms, from the appearance of a celebrity in advertisements for a product...",虛主詞 it 代表的即是名人品牌活動,譯作中文時,因應語詞通順需要,可再重複運用。

2. 中英文敘事方式不同,由於此文本要強調的重點是名人代言,服飾與香水相對並不那麼重要,因此譯作中文時,就不像英文原文那樣把服飾與香水倒裝於前來特別強調。

 前輩指點

　　初入翻譯工作領域新手，由於先前可能尚未接過任何案子，手上累積作品有限，通常只能從各發案方處想辦法得到試稿機會，若華山論劍般比劃，最後由發案方決定合作對象，其實有志以翻譯為職志的新手，除了尋求試稿機會外，若能加入一些相關的專業團體，或是取得相關證照，也可為自己增添不少就業競爭力。

　　據知，目前台灣為培養翻譯人才，從民國 96 年起就已有「中英文翻譯能力檢定考試」，並且自民國 102 年後改由財團法人語言訓練中心擔任主辦單位，專事筆譯與口譯的檢定考試，合格後發予證書。此方面的認證正朝向穩定與完整的方向上繼續發展中。另亦有台北市翻譯業職業工會與台北市翻譯商業同業公會等兩職業組織，皆可為翻譯從業者提供相關資源。以筆者個人經驗為例，當初在通過澳洲的翻譯協會認證考試拿到翻譯師證照後，名字即可列入協會組織會員名冊中，這對接案而言是絕對有正面效益的。

主題 1
廣告 1-4

 英中對照

In the Internet era, the shift from the selling channel to the Internet endangers the need for website promotion. More and more online advertisements are appearing, and online advertising tactics like SEO, SEM, PPC are well known by most Internet advertisers.

Search engine optimization (SEO) is the process of affecting the visibility of a website or a web page in a search engine's unpaid results. Generally, the higher ranked on the search page, the more frequently sites are visited. SEO considers the actual search terms or keywords typed into search engines and which search engines are preferred by their target audience. It is usually implemented by website developers or administrators. They match and do the best to meet the above criteria to achieve the best result without paying anything. The outcome is highly related to the search engine's algorithm which cannot be fully controlled by website developers or administrators.

Pay per click (PPC), contrary to SEO, is a form of paid online advertising and also called cost per click (CPC). It is the most used method to direct traffic to websites, in which advertisers pay the publisher when the ad is clicked. Bid for keywords is a well-known and often used PPC for advertisers in Taiwan. The biggest keyword ads agent, Yahoo, grabbed sales value at NTD 500 million in 2009. Although the trend continues to go up, some potential risk caused by competitors' malicious clicks might possibly lead the industry to collapse. Some advertisers have found their advertising budget is deducted very quickly due to malicious clicks from competitors. They may lose NTD20,000 to NTD30,000 monthly or even more. Two major search engines Google and Yahoo in Taiwan have taken action to prevent this kind of attack, but it seems it cannot be 100% eliminated due to technology changes and advances as time goes by.

中文

　　網路時代，銷售通路轉至網際網路，產生了對網站的促銷需求，越來越多的網路廣告出現，使得大部分網路廣告主也熟知一些可運用的廣告技巧如搜尋引擎優化、搜尋引擎行銷及點擊付費等。

　　搜尋引擎優化（SEO）是種影響網站或網頁在搜尋引擎免費結果頁的可見度程序，一般來說，在搜尋結果頁評比排越高的，就表示有越多的拜訪者。搜尋引擎優化是以搜尋引擎的目標族群喜好及其打入的搜尋字串或關鍵字來判定的，通常由網站管理員或是開發者來執行其優化，他們會針對各篩選條件配對並執行出最佳結果，且不需花費任何費用。這優化的結果與搜尋引擎本身的運算法高度相關，網站管理員或是開發者無法完全掌控。

　　每點擊付費（PPC），不同於搜尋引擎優化，是一種收費網路廣告，也被稱作 CPC，是最常使用的將流量導入網站的網路廣告模式，每當廣告被點選時，廣告主便付費給網站發行者。點擊付費廣告中，台灣廣告主們最熟知關鍵字競標，也常運用它來進行行銷。最大網路廣告代理商 Yahoo 在 2009年時就達到了 50 億元產值，趨勢雖一直在成長，但仍有潛在危機存在，競爭者的惡意點擊，將有可能使業界走向崩壞局面。部分廣告主發現它們投入的廣告預算，因為競爭者的惡意點擊，很快就被扣光，每月可能有 2 萬元至 3 萬元甚至更多的損失產生。國內兩大搜尋引擎 Google 與 Yahoo 雖針對此攻擊已採取防範措施，但似乎看來因為科技與時俱進，也無法百分百完全屏除這類攻擊。

單字片語解釋

- Search engine optimization（SEO）搜尋引擎最佳化

- algorithm　*n.*　運算法、演算法則
  Different algorithms are applied to different search engines.
  不同的搜尋引擎使用不同的演算法則。

- pay per click（PPC）關鍵字廣告；每點擊付費

- contrary to　*adj.*　相反的、對立的
  Mary's viewpoint is contrary to mine.
  瑪莉與我的觀點相反。

- malicious　*adj.*　惡意的
  Jack was blackmailed by a malicious widow who he met a long time ago.
  傑克接到一位多年前認識的惡毒寡婦恐嚇。

- eliminate　*v.*　屏除、淘汰
  Our team was eliminated from the competition in the semi-finals.
  我們的隊伍在準決賽中遭到淘汰。

🔍 相關句型翻譯要點

1. 此文的 SEO，SEM，PPC 及 HTML 等均為專有名詞，若有特定譯名皆須譯出，若是十分普遍常見的譯名，可不需再加註原文，否則第一次出現於文中時須以原括弧號引註原文，其後則以一名表示即可。若在無固有譯名情況下，則直接以原文譯出。

2. 英文常在句子中使用被動語態，但譯為中文時，並不需要將被動態強調出來，反而直譯就好，如第一段原文 "the need for website promotion. More and more online advertisements are appearing, and online advertising tactics like SEO, SEM, PPC are well known by most Internet advertisers..." 並不譯作「對網站促銷的需求被產生」或是「越來越多的網路廣告技巧如搜尋引擎優化、搜尋引擎行銷及點擊付費被廣大廣告主熟知」，而是順譯為「…產生了對網站的促銷需求」及「…大部分網路廣告主也熟知一些可運用的廣告技巧如搜尋引擎優化…」。

3. 原 文 "Generally, the higher ranked on the search page, the more frequently sites are visited." 是「the 比較級 + the 比較級（越…越…）」的句型，此句型很常見到，當中可以是形容詞比較級，也可以是副詞比較級。第一句相當於條件從句。通常會翻作「越…越…」，因此譯作「在搜尋結果頁評比排**越高**的，就表示有**越多**的拜訪者」。

前輩指點

相較於以往，現在翻譯工作者接案來源已經顯得比較多元，可以透過很多直接管道與發案方直接接觸，不須經過翻譯社或是其他組織間接接洽連繫。幾個國內的人力網站，目前也都另闢專門的外包站，專門提供服務給自由工作者或是正職工作者尋找外包接案副業，讓他們可以運用現成平台來找尋案源。國外亦有不少專業翻譯網站可運用，但可能接案者來源來自世界各地，競爭者亦不少，一般而言這些相關平台均會要求繳交一定比例的服務費用，才會提供發案方的直接連絡資料，但要知道的是，取得聯絡資料直接連絡上案主並不保證就一定能拿到案子，因為也有其他同你一樣的接案者與發案方連絡上，而你並不知道這樣的接案者有多少人。

建議有心想在翻譯這條路上行久並成主要工作的朋友，多多灑網，在開始此職涯尚未累積足夠數量的作品與經驗之初，可多瀏覽各平台接案，多闢接案來源，為往後鋪路奠基。

主題 2
藝術 2-1

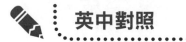 英中對照

Flamenco, is the most representative of Spanish culture. The word flamenco originally is a derivative of "fire" or "flame", as it is connected to the "Cante" and the dance's strong, passionate and solemn nature. The word flamenco may have come to be used for certain behavior in general, which could possibly have come to be applied to the Gitano players and performers.

Flamenco is a genre of music and dance native to the southern Spanish regions of Andalusia, Extremadura and Murcia. It includes cante (singing), toque (guitar playing), baile (dance) and jaleo, which refers to the vocalizations and rhythmic sounds of palmas (handclapping) and pitos (finger snapping). First mentioned in literature in 1774, the genre is thought to have grown out of Andalusian music and dance styles. Although Flamenco is often associated with the gitanos (Romani people of Spain) and a significant proportion of famous flamenco artists are of this ethnicity, the fusion of the various cultures that have coexisted in southern Spain is clearly perceptible in Flamenco music. There are many theories on its origin, and the most widespread highlights a Morisco heritage, with the cultural melting pot that was Andalusia at the time (Andalusians, Muslims, Castilian settlers, Gypsies and Jews) fostering its development over time.

"Carmen" is the most famous flamenco dance drama in the 20th century, it was inspired by George Bizet's great musical interpretation. With the radical rhythm and passionate melody, it brings authenticity to Carmen's damned character and sensual image. The dance drama has become the most convincing interpretation of Carmen on stage.

In recent years, flamenco has become popular all over the world and is taught in many countries, especially in the United States and Japan. In Japan, there are more flamenco academies than there are in Spain. On November 16, 2010, UNESCO (United Nations Education Scientific and Cultural Organization) declared flamenco one of the Masterpieces of the Oral and Intangible Heritage of Humanity.

中文

　　佛朗明哥，是最具代表性的西班牙文化產物。佛朗明哥一字是從火或火焰衍生而來，與歌舞強烈的、熱情的、隆重的天性相連結，現在一般將此字使用於特定行為，像是吉他手及表演者。

　　佛朗明哥是安達魯西亞南西班牙區域、埃斯特雷馬杜拉區、墨西亞區的一種本土音樂及舞蹈，包含了清唱（cante）、吉他伴奏（toque）、舞蹈（baile）與喧鬧聲（Jaleo）。喧鬧聲在此指的是有節奏韻律的擊掌（palmas）與彈指（fitos）聲響或人聲，於 1774 年時首見於文學作品中，此類型藝術被認定為發展出安達魯西亞音樂與舞蹈形式的起源。雖然佛朗明哥通常與西班牙的羅馬人（gitonos）相關，且有特定比例的著名佛朗明哥藝術家們也源於此種族，但我們仍可清楚的在佛朗明哥音樂中，體現辨識出共存於南西班牙區域的多元文化融合。其實關於佛朗明哥起源的理論很多，最廣為流傳的是摩里斯科人遺跡，當時可說是個安達魯西亞文化融爐，融合了安達魯西亞人、回教徒、卡斯提爾人、吉普賽人與猶太人，並經過長時間的涵養而來。

　　《卡門》是二十世紀來最有名的佛朗明哥舞劇，是由比才的歌劇佳作《卡門》啟發而來，藉著強烈的韻律節奏與熱情的音樂旋律，將卡門受爭議的特質與淫蕩形象如實演譯，此舞劇可說是關於卡門故事中最具說服力的舞台表演。

　　近幾年佛朗明哥在世界各地受到歡迎，很多國家都在教授，特別在美國與日本。日本有比西班牙還多的佛朗明哥學院。2010 年的 11 月 16 日，UNESCO（聯合國教育科學暨文化組織）更宣布，佛朗明哥為口頭與無形人文遺產中的傑作。

單字片語解釋

- derivative　*n.*　衍生物；派生物
These compounds are nitrosohydroxylamine derivatives.
這類合成物是亞硝基羥胺衍生物。

- solemn　*adj.*　隆重的
He made a solemn promise to do better.
他鄭重保證要做得更好。

- Andalusia　*n.*　安達魯西亞（西班牙南部區域）

- Gitano　*n.*　西班牙的羅馬人

- perceptible　*adj.*　感知的，可察覺的；可辨的
These changes were already perceptible before the war.
這些變化在戰前就已經感覺得出來了。

1
翻譯技巧

2
主題範例

相關句型翻譯要點

1. 原文 "...it includes cante (singing), toque (guitar playing), baile (dance) and jaleo, which ..." 當中的 it，指的就是主詞佛朗明哥，承接前面句子已有譯出，此處便做省略，以求譯出文句通順清楚。

2. 本文中原文有幾處西班牙語詞，後接有圓括弧英文註釋，當譯為中文時，需針對英文譯為中文，而原西班牙文詞則改為圓括弧註釋方式呈現。如 cante、toque、baile、jaleo 等。

3. 原文 "Although Flamenco is often associated with the gitanos... clearly perceptible in Flamenco music." 使用了 although，通常此用法翻作中文時，有「雖然…但是…」之轉折語意，因此我們須將此語意在文中譯出：「**雖然**」佛朗明哥通常與西班牙的羅馬人 (gitonos) 相關，且有……「**但**」我們仍可清楚的在佛朗明哥音樂中，體現辨識出共存於南西班牙區域的多元文化融合。

★ 前輩指點

　　由於此篇文章恰巧描述主題為西班牙的佛朗明哥藝術，出處並不是英美等地，而是歐洲的西班牙，不少的原文字詞是西班牙文而不是英文，也許查找傳統英漢或英英字典會查不到。建議應先查西英字典，或是利用網路搜尋，先對相關背景有初步了解，再進行譯文動作。

　　另外，針對篇幅較長並參雜多重描述子句的段落，建議可先譯出重點字後，多看幾次句子，前後文拆解融合後，再做最後潤飾以完成譯文。有些時候埋首書案數個小時一直困在同一處時，也可先擱置，過幾天後再回來看，就能譯出更通順的文章了。

　　以本文為例，雖說是以敘述為主，但中間卻雜有很多附加描述及專有名詞，篇幅頗長，需要花點時間反覆讀，以單句讀、以整段落讀，充分了解文意後再來進行譯文，才能盡量趨近完善。

主題 **2**

藝術 2-2

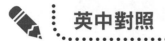 英中對照

Sculpture is a kind of visual art that operates in three dimensions. Its processes originally used carving and modeling, in various forms of materials, such as stone, metal, ceramics, wood etc. Since it shifts as modernism blooms, the process and medium used is almost completely free and not fixed in any setting. More and more non-traditional forms of sculpture, including sound sculpture, light sculpture, environmental art, environmental sculpture, kinetic sculpture, land art, and site-specific art have been added into the sculpture art stream. It is an important form of public art nowadays.

Ju Ming, born in 1938, is the most famous master among Taiwanese sculpture artists, and has earned the most acclaim around the world. He learned wooden sculpture with Lee Chin-Chuan from 1953 to 1957, and continued to learn modern sculpture with Yang Yuyu from 1926 to 1997. He gradually upgraded traditional wooden sculpture into sculpture artworks filled with life meanings based on his simplistic nature and brilliant talent. His works widely and deeply touched most people in Taiwan and gradually caught the attention of western society. There are three famous series of his artworks, which are Nativist series, Taichi series, and Living World series.

Nativist series mainly merge with the affection of native and traditional culture, and it takes buffalo, farm animals and historical personages as major themes. Taichi series is the combination of human and natural environment. It presents aesthetic perception in both visual and design appearance; balanced well with the eastern style of mechanics and aesthetics. The spirits and momentum is expressed extremely. These are Ju Ming's most famous and popular works. A respect for the existing structures of nature is also inherent in the spirit of Taichi.

Ju Ming developed Living World series when he studied in New York in the 1980s. He started working on collages, pottery, stone sculptures and the recent stainless steel series. All of them are focused on humans. This series was inspired by Pop art, and it describes the look of common people. Every creature has his own personality and expression, and all of them are content with the life they have.

In 1999, Ju Ming established Juming Museum in Taipei. The museum stores most of his collections and contributes to the field of art and society a lot. Two main ideas of Ju Ming's viewpoint, "art is the practice of moral teachings" and "to plant art's seed into the hearts" continue to keep him devoted to the road of art.

中文

　　雕塑是在三度空間操作的一種視覺藝術。雕塑過程原本是在石頭、金屬、陶瓷、木材及其他原料上，使用雕刻及塑形技法。但自從現代主義盛行以來，雕塑過程及原料的轉變已經趨向於幾乎完全自由，越來越多非傳統型式雕刻已加入主流雕塑行列。包含了聲音雕塑、光雕塑、環境藝術、環保雕塑、動力學雕塑品、大地藝術、場域特定藝術。雕塑是當今重要的公共藝術之一。

　　朱銘，生於 1938 年，是台灣雕塑家中最有名的大師，並在世界上享有相當高評價，他在 1953 年至 1957 年間，從師李金川學木雕，並在 1926 年至 1997 年間從師楊英風學習現代雕塑。他秉持自身純樸天性與卓越天賦，逐漸地將傳統木雕晉升成富有生命意義的藝術品，作品廣泛地且深深地感動了台灣大眾，並也漸漸引起西方社會的關注。他有三大著名系列作品，鄉土系列、太極系列及人間系列。

　　鄉土系列主要融合了對本土及傳統文化的情感，以水牛、農場動物及歷史人物為主題。太極系列是人類與自然環境的結合，呈現了視覺及設計美感，並平衡了東方力與美，將精神與氣勢表達至極致。太極系列是朱銘最有名且最受歡迎的作品，對既存自然結構的尊敬也蘊含在這太極精神中。

　　朱銘在 1980 年代在紐約學習時，開始發展人間系列，他也開始拼貼、陶器、石雕與近期的不鏽鋼雕塑系列，全都以人為主。此系列靈感來自普普藝術，描述的是一般人的樣子，每個創作物件都有它自身的個性與表情，而人物自身也滿足於它們現有生活中。

　　朱銘在 1999 年時於台北成立的朱銘美術館，收藏了他大部分的作品，並且也對藝術教育及社會貢獻良多。朱銘仍持續秉持他的兩大主要藝術觀，「藝術即修行」及「在心田中種下藝術種子」，繼續致力於美術道路上。

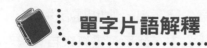 **單字片語解釋**

- carving   *n.*   雕刻；雕刻術；雕刻品
  All the furniture in the room had much carving.
  房間裡所有家具上都有許多雕刻。

- ceramics   *n.*   陶瓷
  Those ceramics are beautiful.
  那些陶器很好看。

- kinetic   *adj.*   動能的；動力學的
  There exist many sources of energy both potential and kinetic.
  那存在著許多勢能和動能的能源。

- nativist   *n.*   本土文化保護者
  She was a famous nativist in the town.
  她是鎮上知名的本土文化保護者。

- merge   *v.*   融合
  Twilight merged into total darkness.
  暮色漸漸沒入黑暗。

- content with 滿足於
  She seemed content with her life as a rich man's playmate.
  她似乎滿足於做有錢男子的玩物。

- moral　*adj.*　道德的、精神的

John is giving her moral support for her loss in families.

約翰對她家庭的損失給予精神支持

- devote　*v.*　致力於、將…奉獻於

Emily devotes herself to the religious activities.

愛蜜莉全心奉獻於宗教活動上。

1

翻譯技巧

2

主題範例

🔍 相關句型翻譯要點

1. 第二段中，年代、數字、日期等譯文皆以阿拉伯數字表示，一般不列出
   「西元」，但若文章來源是史料、研究文件或官方文件時，西元則須譯
   出。此段文字，我們就不特別說「朱銘生於西元 1938 年」，而僅是譯出
   「朱銘生於 1938 年」。同樣的，"...with Lee Chin-Chuan from 1953
   to 1957,..." 與 "...with Yang Yuyu from 1926 to 1997." 也不說「西
   元 1953 年至西元 1957 年」與「西元 1926 年至西元 1997 年」，僅說
   「1953 年至 1957 年」與「在 1926 年至 1997 年間」。

⭐ 前輩指點

　　此篇文章不算是結構複雜的文章，除了有比較多的補述解釋，從技法、本質、沿革等面來更一步補充說明「雕塑」，並沒有牽涉太多複雜的句型。除了注意一些倒裝句型，轉折語氣特殊用法之外，我們其實也可運用標點符號的一些隱形效果，分開太長或較多的補述句，以達到「說清楚」的目標。如分號「；」及冒號「：」，即是頗為實用的標點符號之一。

　　此外，中文常會用的一些連字詞，像是「並且、但是、而、則是…」等，也會常常拿來增加語句的連結性與通順度，是將詞語更增加活性度的好工具。建議初稿譯出後，反覆讀誦，你可以再依語句通順程度，適當加入一些連字詞，讓行文更為出色，讀起來鏗鏘有條理。

主題 2
藝術 2-3

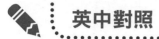 英中對照

There are numerous forms of creative expression in painting, like drawing, gesture, composition, narration, or abstraction. Practitioner's expression and conceptual tendency usually can be seen from their work, and it can be classified into styles that refer to the distinctive visual elements, techniques and methods of the artist or the movement the artist is associated with.

Cubism is the most influential art movement of the 20th century among several modern arts, such as Abstract expressionism, Color Field, and Lyrical Abstraction. It revolutionized European painting and sculpture, and inspired related movements in music, literature, and architecture. Cubism painting is characterized by geometric figures. Painters analyze the subject and break it up into a geometric abstract form. These geometrical figures are normally viewpoints of the subject from various angles. Cubist paintings range from partially abstract to fully abstract.

Pablo Picasso was a Spanish artist and he was one of the pioneers of Cubism. He created artwork not only in painting, but also in sculpture, ceramics etc. through his long lifetime. His career can be divided into several periods. His representative work, Les

Demoiselles d'Avignon, created in 1907, inspired by African artifacts, can be taken as a milestone for stepping into cubism after the Blue Period (1901-1904) and the Rose Period (1904-1906). During Analytic cubism period (1909-1912), Picasso took apart objects and "analyzed" them in terms of their shapes. Later in Synthetic cubism period (1912-1919), cubism developed further to use new elements, cut paper fragments- often wallpaper or portions of newspaper pages in works. It was also the first use of collage fine art.

Picasso started to apply multiple styles to his painting, and he also attempted to make metal sculptures from the 1930s. His most famous work, Guernica, inspired by the German bombing of Guernica during the Spanish Civil War was completed in 1937. It denounced the inhumanity, brutality and hopelessness of war. Picasso still kept his abundant ingenuity in various forms of art towards the end of his career though he has attained remarkable achievement in the world of art. There is no other artist who surpasses Picasso in wielding influence in the 20th century. He definitely is the greatest artist of the 20th century.

中文

　　繪畫有多種的創作表達方式，如描繪姿態、解構構圖、記述或是抽象。繪畫從事者的表現手法及概念傾向通常可由其畫作看出，也可藉由特別視覺元件、技巧及方法，或是與藝術家的流派，區分出不同的畫風。

　　立體派藝術是 20 世紀數種現代藝術如抽象畫派、色面繪畫、抒情抽象畫派中最具影響力的。立體派藝術改革了歐洲的繪畫及雕塑，並在音樂、文學及建築方面啟發了相關的運動。立體派最明顯的特徵是幾何圖形的使用，立體派畫家分析物體，並且將其解構成幾何圖形，這些圖形通常是從不同角度看物體的視角，立體派畫作有部分抽象，也有的是完全抽象。

　　西班牙藝術家巴勃羅・畢卡索是立體派的先驅之一，他一生不只有繪畫創作，更有雕塑及陶瓷等藝術作品。他的創作成品據估有 5 萬件，創作生涯可分做數個時期，最具代表性的作品—亞維儂姑娘，是在 1907 年受到非洲藝術品的啟發完成，可說是畢卡索在經歷過 1901 至 1904 年的藍色時期，與 1904 至 906 年的粉紅色時期後，進入立體派時期的里程碑。在 1909 至 1912 年間的分析立體派時期，畢卡索將物體分開，並從它們的形狀分析它們，接著在 1912 至 1919 年間的綜合立體派時期，進一步發展將新元素紙，通常是海報紙或報紙，切成碎片，運用在畫作上。這也是拼貼藝術的初次使用。

　　從 1930 年起，畢卡索開始在畫作上展現多種風格，同時也嘗試創作金屬雕塑。他在 1937 年完成的名作《格爾尼卡》，乃是由西班牙內戰中德國轟炸格爾尼卡激發而來，譴責了戰爭的殘忍、暴虐與無望。即使畢卡索已在藝術界獲得非凡成就，但他一直到生涯後期仍持續以豐沛創造力創作不同形式的藝術作品。20 世紀沒有其他人超越畢卡索，擁有如此大的影響力，他絕對是 20 世紀最偉大的藝術家之一。

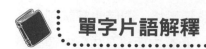 **單字片語解釋**

- composition　　*n.*　　構成；構圖；成分
  We examined the rock trying to figure out its composition.
  我們檢驗了這一石塊，想弄清它的構成成分。

- narration　　*n.*　　敘述，講述；記述體
  A biography is a form of narration.
  傳記是一種記敘文。

- inspire　　*v.*　　啟發、賦予⋯靈感
  The blue sky inspires the painter.
  那片藍色天空啟發了畫家的靈感。

- geometric　　*adj.*　　幾何（學）的
  Her dress is made of geometric figures.
  她那件洋裝是由幾何圖形構成的。

- collage　　*n.*　　拼貼美術
  This artwork includes comics and collages.
  這作品包含了漫畫及拼貼。

- denounce　*v.*　指責
  Mary denounced Jason as a traitor at the meeting.
  瑪莉在會中指責傑森是叛徒。

- wield　*v.*　行使（權力）、施加（影響）
  Peter was nominally the leader, but his mother is actually the one who wielded the power.
  彼得名義上是領導，但實際握權的其實是他母親。

🔍 相關句型翻譯要點

1. 原文 "Cubism is the most influential art movement of the 20th century among several modern arts, such as .... It revolutionized European painting and sculpture, and inspired related movements... and architecture." 中 It 其實也指的就是主詞 Cubsism，我們譯作中文時，可以依語意及通順需求，再重複使用於文中。

2. 原文 "He created artwork not only in painting, but also in sculpture, ceramics etc. through his long lifetime." 中的 not only... but also 有「不但（僅）…也…」之意，譯作中文時，此意必須譯出。

3. 原 文 "During Analytic cubism period (1909-1912), Picasso took apart objects and "analyzed" them in terms of their shapes. Later in Synthetic cubism period (1912-1919), cubism developed further to use new elements, cut paper fragments- often wallpaper or portions of newspaper pages in works. It was also the first use of collage fine art." 中 often wallpaper or portions of newspaper pages 為 cut paper fragment 的補述，補充說明了前述簡短的紙切碎片，在此用標點符號連字號 - 的方式處理，比較不會出現過於冗長句子結構，模糊了讀者重點。

⭐ 前輩指點

　　一般而言，原文若為敘述或描述某一概念、事物的介紹文章，通常句型及文章架構應不太複雜，有可能有數個結構相同的句子串成整段文字，在翻譯時，同樣的架構模式可以一併採用，差別只是在於將特定詞語翻譯成中文時的用字遣詞。同意思的字詞很多，譯者的「推敲」份際，就依經驗值而言，會有不同的呈現。

　　如本文為敘述文介紹立體派繪畫藝術及畢卡索，段落多為重複的簡單結構句子所構成，譯出時也就不大需要運用太多解構與重組，很明確地直譯，頂多在擇字時，需仔細查找此領域內特殊用詞或已沿用許久，相沿成習的特殊詞語。

主題 **2**

藝術 2-4

 英中對照

It is common to point out Victorian Architecture when we discuss western architecture. Victorian architecture refers to the various styles of houses built in the reign of Queen Victoria (1837-1901), which includes Gothic Revival, Italianate, Folk Victorian, and Victorian Queen Anne. It brings an enormous influence to modern architecture and is the base of modern architecture.

This style is generally elegantly designed, and it reflects the inner structure from the exterior. There are different features incorporated in different styles that are categorized as the period changes. Gothic Revival style adopts elements that most ecclesiastical buildings have. It utilizes stone as the main building materials; features such as pointed arches, rib vaults, tall towers and flying buttresses are common to Gothic Revival style architecture.

Italianate style is also called bracketed style, and it includes features like flat roofs, cornices, and bay windows. Folk Victorian buildings usually appear as L shapes or square shapes, and they are decorated with spindle shaped decorations in the front porch. The eaves are supported with brackets. The Victorian Queen Anne style is featured with surrounding verandas, round towers or polygonal spire, bay windows, pretty colorful pattern decorated walls and chimney pots.

So called "the empire on which the sun never sets", the British Empire ruled all over the world. Victorian architecture spread to the world as well. There is much famous Victorian architecture outside the United Kingdom. In Germany, Hohe Domkirche St. Petrus represents a Gothic Revival style building. There is much Victorian architecture in the United States and Australia as well. Government House, Melbourne is one of the Italianate style buildings. Hong Kong was once a British colony that also holds several Victorian architectures such as Murray house in Stanley. It is the oldest surviving European Victorian building in Hong Kong. It was built of giant granites, and combined with both western and eastern characteristics. It not only contains Greek's cromlech but also adopts Chinese top roofs, which demonstrates its uniqueness.

No matter which style the Victorian building is, different exteriors and materials all reflect advanced development in architectural history. The value cannot be easily ignored.

中文

　　當我們在討論西方建築時，常會提到維多利亞式（Victorian）建築，維多利亞式房屋泛指英國維多利亞女王在位時（1840-1900）所出現的多種住宅風格，包含了哥德式復興（Gothic Revival）、義大利式（Italianate）、平民維多利亞式（Folk Victorian）和女王安妮式（Victorian Queen Anne），此一風格影響現代建築甚鉅，算是現代建築的基礎。

　　此一風格大體上設計精美，從外型反映內部結構，隨著時間沿革而細分的各式建築，各有不同的強調重點，歌德復興式偏重採用了以往歐洲大教堂的建築元素，有較多石材的應用，還有尖拱、交叉拱、高塔、飛扶壁等常見特徵。

　　義大利式風格也叫支架（bracketed）風格，具有平屋頂、飛簷及有角的凸窗等特徵；平民維多利亞式房屋通常是 L 形的或正方形，常在前門廊用很多紡錘形的裝飾，屋簷底下加上支架；女王安妮式有繞房門廊、圓塔或多角形尖塔、有角凸窗、牆上有彩色花紋和極其漂亮的裝飾物、石板瓦或陶瓦屋頂，及煙囪。

1
翻譯技巧

2
主題範例

　　隨著「日不落國」英國強大殖民主權四散至世界各地，維多利亞式的建築亦大量傳襲至世界各地。在英國本土之外，也有很多著名的各式維多利亞風格建築。德國科隆大教堂，即是歌德復興式建築範例，美國及澳洲也擁有大量維多利亞時期建築，澳洲墨爾本的總督府是義大利式建築例子。鄰近的香港，因曾為英國殖民地，也有維多利亞式建築物，如位於赤柱的美利樓，即是香港碩果僅存的古歐陸維多利亞式建築物。它主要以巨型花崗岩建成，融合了東、西方建築特色，既有仿希臘復古式圓形石柱，又採用了中式的瓦面斜頂屋頂，設計可謂別具特色。

　　維多利亞式建築不管是哪一種風格，外形和用材各異均反映了建築史上在風格、眼界上的巨大進步，價值不容小覷。

單字片語解釋

- Victorian architecture 維多利亞式建築

- reign　　*n.*　　統治；支配
  The reign of a wise ruler benefits his country.
  賢明統治者的統治有益於他的國家。

- revival　　*n.*　　甦醒；復活；復興
  There has been a revival of interest in this composer's music.
  人們對這位作曲家的音樂又重新產生興趣。

- ecclesiastical　　*adj.*　　（基督）教會的、教士的
  This building had once been a part of an ancient ecclesiastical house.
  此建築物曾是一個古老教會房子的一部分。

🔍 相關句型翻譯要點

1. 原文 "It not only contains Greek's cromlech but also adopts Chinese top roofs, which demonstrates its uniqueness." 為 not only... but also「不但…而且…」句型，所以譯句一定要涵蓋此意，翻成「既有仿希臘復古式圓形石柱，又採用了中式的瓦面斜頂屋頂。」

2. 原「隨著日不落國……澳洲墨爾本的總督府是義大利式建築例子。」中文段落純粹描寫闡述各地維多利亞式建築的例子，看不出明顯的時勢差異，但在譯作英文時，則應依各句時態的不同，使用不同時勢語法。故可見到 "...British empire ruled all over the world..."、"... Hong Kong was once a British colony that also holds several Victorian architectures..."

⭐ 前輩指點

　　翻譯進行翻譯工作時，有時因自身學習背景與所執行的翻譯文本身並無關連，翻譯工作者若非有較為廣泛的知識背景基礎，則需要強勁的快速建立背景知識能力，務求能對手上正在進行的翻譯任務主題，有更深入的了解，才能有方法完成此次任務。

　　比方說此文正討論著維多利亞風格建築，譯者本人並無建築相關教育背景，對此範圍所知有限，因此需要尋求一些資源來補不足，一些基本背景知識的需求，可以先查找百科全書，而某些專業領域，就必須查找更專業的辭典或參考書。相信這些資源，能給譯者提供清楚而又立即的背景知識，好幫助譯者能譯出正確文章。

　　一些線上網路資源，如像百科全書般性質的 wikipedia 及 Encyclopaedia Britannica 大英百科全書就是很好的背景知識來源，可為譯者帶來許多便利並增進翻譯效率。

主題 3
觀光 3-1

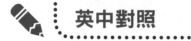
英中對照

There are nearly 200 countries in the world, and they are spread over 7 continents. It is difficult to be aware of every aspect like language, culture and race among these countries. Although people join package tours overseas more frequently, the guide cannot accompany everyone with 24-hour service. Tourists still need to pay attention to some related social customs or taboos in different countries for fear of causing any trouble by accident.

Asia, for example, the most-visited destination for Taiwan tourists, is a region with a vast territory and various races, which impacts on the taboos very much, especially in religious aspects. Some taboos are provided as followed for reference.

In India and Nepal, Hindus take cows as holy animals; therefore, it is prohibited to take photos of cows or to hurt them when driving on the road. Indians express their agreement by shaking their heads instead of nodding, which is unique and acts oppositely to general situations where agreement is expressed by nodding. Nepal is another country which respects cows. Do not discuss issues regarding beef in front of Nepalese. Do use your hand as the cutlery when you dine if the table setting does not include knives and forks. Do use your right hand when you dine because the left hand is considered filthy.

Sri Lanka, is close to India, and Buddhism is the major religion in Sri Lanka though there are small portions of Hindus and Muslims. People in Sri Lanka do not like to be taken as a part of India, and this should be taken into account by tourists.

A large majority of the population in Myanmar practices Buddhism. To show respect for Buddha, it is necessary to remove shoes when you enter temples. It is considered impolite to touch the heads of other people; therefore, do not touch a kid's head. There is a similar taboo in Lao and they believe the head is where the spirit lodges. Never touch a Lao's head.

Buddhism is prevalent in Thailand, and there are rules to govern the religion. Monks obey the doctrine of Hinayana Buddhism. It is prohibited for them to touch a female or be touched by a female. Female tourists should avoid touching monks in public.

Islam is the official religion in Malaysia. Do not disturb Muslims during their evening prayer when you visit Malaysia. It is impolite to point at someone with the index finger, and it is better to use a thumb instead. As in the above situation in other countries, it is impolite to touch a kid's head. Non-Muslim cannot enter a mosque without permission. It is required that shoes be taken off before you go into a mosque. Do not take photos of the people who are praying and do not walk across the front of prayers.

Most Indonesians are Muslim; however, most Balinese believe in Hindu. Some Indonesians consider cameras or flashlights as an instrument to catch the soul of human. It is better to get permission from people whom you wish to photograph.

Japan is a nation with a very strict code of behavior and politeness. Do bring gifts when you visit Japanese friends. It is very important to be on time in Japan. Do not be late when you have an appointment with a Japanese person in order to avoid keeping people waiting.

中文

　　地球七大洲,將近有 200 個國家,語言、文化、種族之多,是無法一一細述瞭解的,但因現在國人常有機會至國外旅遊,即使跟團出遊,導遊不見得能 24 小時隨行照料。因此,對旅遊地點相關風俗禁忌,還是稍有了解較為妥當,以免在不經意間造成困擾。

　　以國人最常出遊的亞洲為例,面積大,種族多,特別是宗教信仰多樣,影響了風俗禁忌甚極,略述一些應注意的風俗禮儀,提供參考。

　　印度、尼泊爾均尊牛為神聖不可侵犯的動物,盡量避免對牛攝影,開車時要注意不可撞到牛。最特別的是,印度人回答問題時若搖頭,其實是表示肯定,而不是我們一般理解的否定,請別會錯意。尼泊爾也是一個重視牛的國家,在尼泊爾人面前應避免談到吃牛肉,如用餐時如果沒擺出刀叉,就表示要以手抓食;但左手代表不潔,應該要使用右手吃飯。

　　鄰近印度的斯里蘭卡,宗教信仰雖以佛教為主,但也有少數印度教、回教徒。斯里蘭卡人不喜歡被誤認為印度的一部分,旅客應多注意。

　　緬甸大多數人口信奉佛教。進入寺廟皆必須脫鞋,以示對佛陀的尊敬。觸摸別人的頭則被認為是無禮的行為,所以別碰觸小孩的頭部。在寮國,他們相信頭部是精靈寄宿的地方,所以也有這樣的禁忌。千萬別碰寮國人的頭。

　　泰國是佛教盛行的國家,有許多保障宗教的條文,僧侶恪遵小乘佛教教義,絕對禁止接觸女性或被女性觸摸,因此女性遊客在公共場合亦應避免碰觸僧侶。

1

翻譯技巧

2

主題範例

馬來西亞國教為回教，應注意在傍晚祈禱時間內不要打擾回教徒。另外，以食指指人是一件不禮貌的行為，最好以拇指代替，觸摸小孩子的頭也是不禮貌的行為。進入清真寺必須脫鞋，非教徒必須先得到寺方准許才可進入；對於正在寺中祈禱的教徒，儘量不拍攝他們的照片，更不能由前方穿過。

印尼人大部分為回教徒，峇里島人則多數信奉印度教，對島國印尼而言，少數民族認為照相或閃光燈是攝人靈魂的器具，拍照前最好應事先徵求被拍攝者的同意。

日本是一個相當多禮的國家，拜訪友人時勿忘攜帶禮物。守時也是日本人非常重視的觀念，與日本人相約千萬別遲到，以免讓人久候。

單字片語解釋

- taboo　*n.*　禁忌、忌諱
  Women are taboo on the ship.
  女人是不准上船的。

- cutlery　*n.*　餐具
  Mary would like to order cutlery as a wedding gift.
  瑪莉想訂購餐具作為婚禮禮物。

- filthy　*adj.*　不潔的、汙穢的
  This movie is full of the filthy language.
  這部電影充滿猥褻語言。

- prevalent　*adj.*　流行的、盛行的、普遍的
  Colds are prevalent in the winter.
  冬天很流行感冒。

- mosque　*n.*　清真寺
  They go to the mosque to pray once a day.
  他們每天去清真寺禱告一次。

相關句型翻譯要點

1. 使用 it 虛主詞代替「細述瞭解各個國家不同的語言、文化、種族多種面向」一事，原中文「但因現在國人常有機會至國外旅遊，即使跟團出遊，導遊不見得能 24 小時隨行照料。」有「雖然現在國人常有機會至國外旅遊…但是導遊不見得能…」之意，所以我們在譯作英文時，使用了 although..., ... 用法，較能凸顯與強調語氣。

2. "...express their agreement by shaking their heads instead of nodding, which is unique and acts oppositely to general situations where agreement is expressed by nodding" 中使用 which 子句來帶出其後的補充解釋，說明所謂的一般情況是如何的，在此一般情況即是點頭表示同意 agreement is expressed by nodding。

3. 「鄰近印度的斯里蘭卡，宗教信仰雖以佛教為主，但也有少數印度教、回教徒。斯里蘭卡人不喜歡被誤認為印度的一部分，旅客應多注意。」有「雖然…但是…」語意在，所以譯作英文時，要將 ...though 句型…翻出。"...Buddhism is the major religion in Sri Lanka though there are small portions of Hindus and Muslims...."

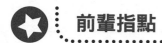

前輩指點

　　新手譯者接案不易，除了翻譯品質要維持一定水準之外，時間進度的掌控是一大挑戰，特別是相對於經驗豐富的老手，時間進度的掌控，更是新手入門時該特別注意的要項。若接的案子是整本書的翻譯，更考驗了譯者的耐性、定力與時間管理的能力。

　　切記一旦確定接案，一定要展現誠懇合作態度，不要拖稿，盡自己最大能力掌握翻譯速度，最忌諱鬧失蹤搞人間蒸發，讓編輯面對難以收拾的局面，破壞了合作關係。都已經是相對比較難接到案子的新手了，難得接到案子，千萬要特別留意職業道德與合作態度，秉持誠懇，避免造成合作編輯或出版社的困擾，才有更長遠的路可走。

　　曾耳聞過比較誇張的例子，有譯者接了案後搞失聯，整整消失了兩到三年的時間才跟編輯聯絡，所以一本書就這樣拖了兩三年才出版。實在是相當負面不可取的，除非是享有聲名的老手或是相關招牌譯手，非得由他來譯，不然我想任何編輯或出版社，都是領人薪水的，可擔不起此類風險啊！切記一旦有了壞名聲，日後要想再接案，難度無形中就更添加好幾分了。

主題 **3**
觀光 3-2

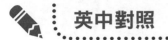

There are more and more tourist attractions that take "bridge" as the theme planned and built recently in Taiwan. Pingtung has constructed a suspension bridge after New Pingtung Sky Bridge and Ping Seto glass suspension bridge opened in Nantou. This just opened bridge has attracted crowds since the recent New Year holiday. The total length of the bridge is 262 meters, and it links Sandimen Township and Machia township. Its height is about 45 meters from the bridge floor to the river bed. It has added luster to Pingtung with new imagery which is decorated with unique aboriginal glaze beads and lights at night.

The local master, Sakuliu Pavavalung designed the bridge by combining elements like glaze beads, aboriginal culture and light. He inlaid the glaze beads, which represent the Payuan and the Drekay on both ends of the bridge. There are also 24 story tablets set up each telling a moving story from the tribes. Tourists can understand indigenous culture and stories further when they walk along the bridge slowly. The lights of the bridge are turned on to bring a romantic atmosphere and reveal a different scene at nightfall.

The bridge has two entrances for Sandimen Township and Machia township, each of them a adopt different design. The Sandimen entrance is decorated with mosaic artworks on the anchorage base and retaining wall by the students in Timur elementary school. The pattern on the anchorage base of Machia entrance was provided by the students in Peiye elementary school. In addition, there is stone installation art set up at both ends. The one at the Machia end represents the "sweet potato", and the other one at Sandimen represents "taro". It is meaningful to symbolize "racial integration" by setting up "sweet potato plus taro" theme. The suspension bridge has been opened since the 26th of December, 2015.

Sandimen and Machia townships in Pingtung maintain the special cultural property of the Payuan and the Drekay. There is a "Taiwan indigenous culture park" in Peiye village of Machhia township, which demonstrates mainly indigenous architecture art, drapery craft, and living styles. The park provides not only craft classes but also indigenous meals. Tourists who visit not only indulge in the pretty natural scene but also get to know indigenous culture.

中文

　　近年來台灣境內相繼有不少以「橋」為主題規畫的旅遊景點，繼南投天空之橋及坪瀨琉璃光之橋後，屏東也有了天空之橋「山川琉璃吊橋」，這座新建造的橋，在新年假期引來參觀人潮。此橋全長 262 公尺，連結了屏東三地門鄉與瑪家鄉北葉村。橋面距離河床平均高度約 45 公尺，以原住民獨特的琉璃珠作為橋身意象，夜晚時更化身為光雕橋樑，為屏東增添了一份新色彩。

　　在地藝術大師撒古流・巴瓦瓦隆設計了此吊橋本體，他結合了琉璃珠意象、原住民文化與光雕藝術，將代表排灣族、魯凱族的琉璃珠鑲嵌於橋的兩側，並設有 24 面故事牌，故事牌述說著部落裡的一個個動人故事。遊客通過橋樑時能夠放慢腳步欣賞，進一步了解原住民故事與文化。入夜後吊橋點亮燈光，更增添浪漫氛圍，展現了另一番不同風情。

　　吊橋兩端分三地門端與瑪家端入口，採取不同設計意象，三地門端由地磨兒國小學生，以馬賽克藝術作品裝置於錨碇座牆面及擋土牆牆面，瑪家端則是由北葉國小學生，提供錨碇座牆面圖案創作。另外兩端還各設置一座巨石裝置藝術，瑪家端是「蕃藷」意象，三地門端是「芋仔」意象，以「芋仔蕃藷」象徵族群融合、不分彼此，相當具有意義，吊橋已於 2015 年 12 月 26 日正式啟用。

　　屏東三地門鄉與瑪家鄉擁有豐富的排灣及魯凱族特殊文化資產，瑪家鄉的北葉村內有一處「台灣原住民族文化園區」，主要展示了台灣原住民族的建築藝術、衣飾工藝與生活型態，不僅完整呈現部落風貌，更提供手工藝教學和原住民風味餐等，讓來到屏東三地門鄉與瑪家鄉的遊客，除了欣賞大自然美景，還可以藉此瞭解原住民文化！

1 翻譯技巧

2 主題範例

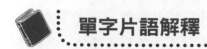 **單字片語解釋**

- suspension bridge 吊橋
  This is the famous suspension bridge in this area.
  這是這區域有名的吊橋。

- glaze bead 琉璃珠
  She wears the necklace with glaze beads to show a unique taste.
  她配戴著琉璃珠項鍊展示特殊品味。

- inlay　*v.*　鑲嵌，嵌入 (inlay, inlaid, inlaid)
  The walls were inlaid with sparkling jewels.
  牆壁鑲著發光的寶石。

- tribe　*n.*　部落
  Everyone in the tribe is equal.
  在部落中的每個人都是平等的。

- indigenous　*adj.*　原住民的、土著的、本土的
  Kangaroos are indigenous to Australia.
  袋鼠原產於澳大利亞。

- drapery　　*n.*　　衣飾、織品

He works in the drapery department of the store.

他在商店的紡織品部工作。

- craft　　*n.*　　工藝、手藝

John is trying to apply modern techniques to this traditional craft.

約翰試圖將現代技術用於這項傳統工業。

1

翻譯技巧

2

主題範例

🔍 相關句型翻譯要點

1. 原中文習慣並無特別時勢趨向，但譯作英文時，當依時勢做句型結構及文法上調整，如 "Pingtung has constructed a suspension bridge after New Pingtung Sky Bridge and Ping Seto glass suspension bridge opened in Nantou...." 的 has constructed 及 "This just opened bridge has attracted crowds since..." 中的 has attracted。同段落中，只是一般時勢描寫橋身事實方面的句子，如橋身本身高度及裝飾等，譯作英文時就以現在式呈現為 "Its height is about 45 meters from the bridge floor to the river bed."。

2. 段落起首兩句主詞是藝術大師，主要在描述他如何設計此橋，翻作英文時依主詞來調整文法及時勢，即成為 "The local master, Sakuliu Pavavalung designed the bridge by combining elements like glaze beads, aboriginal culture and light. He inlaid the glaze beads, which represent the Payuan and the Drekay on both ends of the bridge." 而上譯出句中排灣族與魯凱族的英文譯名，由查證固有譯名而來，不須再附上括號解釋。

前輩指點

　　初接翻譯案件的新手，不管是與翻譯社合作或是自行直接與案主接洽，接案稿費酬勞一般皆不會在原先的期望值以上，通常是在期望值往下扣，因為雙方尚未合作過，對於實際產出內容及過程中所需另外再「加工」的時間或其他成本尚未有基本了解，因此稿費價格上算是「學徒價」。新手譯者應避免太過要求稿費而喪失接案機會，也不需要擔心一路接「低於行情」的案子，之後將永遠淪為辛苦的低廉文字工，接不到合理行情案子。

　　譯者應秉持一個原則，要讓付錢買你專業的人，付錢付得覺得是「值得」的，才是個穩健且長期的翻譯職涯目標與方向。學徒期應以培養實力為主，抱持感謝的心態來接案，感謝案主給予機會，透過無數經驗累積，才能有日後的合理行情價碼可得。

主題 **3**
觀光 3-3

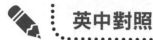
英中對照

Using factory tours as a part of the Public Relations mechanism for business has been practiced for many years. It is an arranged and planned visit to a factory to see the manufacturing process of the product. Recently, as lifestyle in Taiwan changes, people are more willing to spend time and money on recreational activities; factory tours have become a popular activity that is promoted officially and privately by the government and business in order to advance the tourist industry and regenerate traditional manufacturing industry.

Traditional manufacturers, gradually convert themselves to "industrial tourism" or "industry tourism" to enhance profit and business image. Most of them operate their factory like a museum where they utilize their extensive collections, guided tours and informative materials to communicate the business culture and entrepreneurship to the visitors or customers in a learning-through-play environment; therefore, factories are no longer stereotyped places which are hard to get close to.

To assist local industry to get a benefit from tourism, Taiwan's government has actively supported factories by pushing "The Tourism Factory Project" initiated in 2003 and outsourced to the Industrial Technology Research Institute. Later in 2008, an evaluation operation mechanism was established. Candidates undergo several stringent evaluations and assessments, including the factory theme, factory space planning, guided tours and experience facilities, corporate image and promotional material design, as well as the operation model of the tourism factory. There are in total 5 major criteria for the evaluation of tourism factories. Fifty-three model tourism factories from all industries have been successfully selected throughout Taiwan so far.

Different from the tourism factories abroad, tourism factories are more diversified over various industries in Taiwan. Taiwan started tourism factories late, but its unique geographical advantage and local cultural characteristics has brought a fast success since the project's implementation. There are five categories of selected model factories, which are 7 daily necessities, art and humanities, health, food, and living. Some of them are not only popular in Taiwan, but also catch the attention of international tourists, like rice castle, Kuo Yuan Ye Museum of Cake and Pastry, Taiwan Metal Creation Museum, BRAND'S health museum, Republic of chocolate, Taiwan soya-mixed meat museum and Shu Shin Bou Wagashi Museum.

Tourism factories offer traditional industries an alternative for transformation, so as to seek innovation toward sustainability in this competitive era. It truly keeps the hope seeing small and micro enterprises that once generated the Taiwan Economic Miracle once again shine as stars in the sky.

中文

用觀光工廠做為企業的公關機制在歐美已經行之多年，它是安排、計畫好的可以看到產品製造過程的工廠參觀。近年來由於生活型態改變，台灣民眾更願意在休閒活動上花比較多的時間與金錢，觀光工廠遂變成熱門活動，政府官方與民間私人企業為了提升觀光業並再生傳統製造業，大力的推廣觀光工廠。

傳產製造業漸漸地轉化為產業的觀光或是產業觀光以促進企業的獲利能力與企業形象。他們大部分是以博物館的方式來運作工廠，運用廣泛的收集，導覽及豐富資訊素材來對參觀者或顧客進行溝通，讓企業文化或創業精神在「玩中學」的環境被了解與學習，工廠因此不再是個像是以往有著沉重印象而難以親近的地方。

為了幫助地方產業能從觀光中獲益，台灣政府非常積極地推動起始於 2003 年發包給工研院的觀光工廠專案，後來在 2008 年時，評估運作的機制建立完成，它進行數項嚴格的評估與檢查，包含工廠主題、工廠空間規劃、導覽、體驗設施、企業形象、文宣品設計及觀光工廠的營運模式，有五項主要的評估原則，目前為止已有從不同產業選出的模範觀光工廠 53 家。

　　有別於國外的觀光工廠，台灣的觀光工廠相當分散於各種產業中，雖然起步晚，但特殊的地理優勢與在地文化特徵卻使得計畫推動順利，快速成功。獲選的模範工廠共有五種類別，分別是藝術人文超歡樂、開門七件事、居家生活超幸福、醇酒美食超級讚、健康美麗超亮眼等。當中有些工廠不只在台灣熱門，同時也吸引了國際觀光客的注意力，像中興穀堡稻米博物館、郭元益糕餅博物館、台灣金屬創意館、白蘭氏健康博物館、宏亞巧克力共和國、台灣滷味博物館、手信坊創意和果子文化館等。

　　觀光工廠替傳統產業提供了轉型方案，讓傳產在此競爭激烈的年代能尋求創新與永續，誠摯希望曾發光發熱帶起台灣經濟奇蹟的中小企業能夠像天空中的繁星再次閃亮。

1
翻譯技巧

2
主題範例

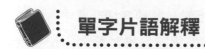

單字片語解釋

- mechanism   *n.*   機制、結構
  The mechanism of the clock is very complicated.
  這個鐘的機件結構很複雜。

- regenerate   *v.*   使再生、使新生、改造
  Nails are constantly regenerating.
  指甲不斷地新生。

- entrepreneurship   *n.*   創業精神、企業精神
  Young people are enthusiastic about entrepreneurship.
  年輕人對於創業興致很高。

- learning-through-play 從玩中學

- stringent   *adj.*   嚴格的
  This machine demands stringent specification.
  這台機器要求高標準。

- criteria　*n.*　原則、標準
  Peter describes several important design criteria.
  彼得提出了幾條重要的設計原則。

- alternative　*n.*　替代方案、可採用的方法
  One of the alternatives that open to you is to quit.
  其中一個你可以選擇的替代方案，就是辭職。

🔍 相關句型翻譯要點

1. 由於觀光工廠的創新方式營造出的「玩中學」增加了親和感，讓接近與瞭解比較容易進行，這是有「因果」關係的句子，我們使用連接副詞 therefore 來表達，其前是前一句子的分號，其後接逗號為「;therefore,」，用以連接句義上的前一句是因，而後一句 factories are no longer stereotyped places which are hard to get close to. 是果。

2. 「為了幫助地方產業能從觀光中獲益，台灣政府非常積極地推動起始於 2003 年發包給工研院的觀光工廠專案⋯」，「為了⋯」有表目的意涵，所以我們運用 in order to，它的正式用法為 in order to + V = to + V，更明確的說，in order to + V 的功能為副詞，用來修飾其前或其後的動詞；而 to + V（不定詞）在句子中則可作為名詞、形容詞或副詞使用。

3. "Some of them are not only popular in Taiwan, but also catch the attention of international tourists..." 此為 not only...but also... 句型，須把「不僅⋯而且⋯」的意思翻出，所以譯出「當中有些工廠不只在台灣熱門，同時也吸引了國際觀光客的注意力」。

⭐ 前輩指點

　　不管是出版社或是直接的發案主，在確定接案譯者前，通常會給所有潛在接案者試譯機會，試譯是編輯測試譯者的翻譯能力，同時也是譯者測試和編輯間磁場是否契合的機會。若是案子為書籍的翻譯，很可能試譯的題目就是擷取某一段內容，約定於某個時間點前交給編輯，這樣最能篩選出最符合出版社或發案方要求的譯者，不僅在翻譯能力上，立於相同條件做比較，更對完成度方面有前測參考值，日後對翻譯日程的時間掌控，也比較能明確控制。

　　通常就跟一般找工作的情形一樣，送出試譯稿後，若等一段時間沒有進一步消息，譯者可以積極的主動聯繫詢問後續，以表達自己對翻譯工作的熱忱，當然，詢問信要有方法與技巧，要能適當的表現出自己的態度又不失禮貌，要能表達關心又不顯得是在催促，才不會讓編輯覺得反感被打擾，變成拒絕往來戶就得不償失了。字的表達和善解人意對譯者而言很重要，連這試譯之後的詢問信，也是文字能力的體現，不可不慎。

主題 3
觀光 3-4

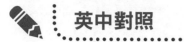

英中對照

Night markets or night bazaars are a unique tourism activity in Asian countries compared with Western society. Street markets operated at night usually have more entertainments, such as eating and shopping than day market. They are typically open-air markets.

Most night markets exist in Asian countries or areas with a Chinese culture background, such as Taiwan, Singapore, Malaysia, China, Thailand, and Chinatowns worldwide. Taiwan, for example, is regarded as one of the world's top destinations for food lovers. It holds several famous night markets which attract food lovers to enjoy the food. A recent online poll by a local website has ranked the top 10 night markets in northern Taiwan. Ningxia night market is the no. 1 at this poll. Ningxia is known as a veritable heaven for traditional snack foods such as pig liver soup, egg yolk taro cake, and zhi gao fan (rice with pig's feet).

The focus of night markets in other countries might not be the food compared with Taiwan. They actually bring together a collection of stalls that usually sell goods such as fruit, vegetables, snacks, toys, clothes, movie discs and ornaments at cheap or reasonable prices. It is common to see haggling over prices at such markets. For example, Chiang Mai Night Bazaar, one of the most popular attractions in Chiang Mai, Thailand, is known for its handicrafts and portrait paintings. There are also jewelry, toys, clothing, and high tech items such as CDs and DVDs. Although the initial price is cheaper there, compared with other countries bargaining with the store keeper is needed to get the best value of the goods.

Apart from Chinatowns worldwide, there are few night markets that exist in western society. Cairns Night Markets & Food Court is one of them. It is the first Night Market in Australia. It started with an open market in 1991 and developed further into an indoor market with 130 stalls currently. There are licensed restaurants, food courts, Chinese massages, etc. It operates every day from 5pm in the Night Market or 10am in the Food Court till late. It never closes.

Night markets are not only a place to enjoy food, but also a hot spot to experience cultural aspects of local daily life no matter where you go especially in Asia. Tourists should not give up the opportunity to explore them.

中文

　　與西方社會相比，夜市是亞洲國家特有的觀光活動，是在晚上運作的街頭市集，通常有比白天市集還多的娛樂，如飲食、購物，它通常是在開放場所運作的市集。

　　夜市大部分都是亞洲國家如台灣、新加坡、馬來西亞、泰國，或是在世界各地的中國城才有。以世界知名美食愛好者最嚮往的台灣為例，就有好幾個吸引美食愛好者前去品嚐享用美食的知名夜市。近期一項當地網站作的線上投票就選出了北台灣十大夜市，寧夏夜市在這次投票中脫穎而出成了第一名，它真的是個傳統點心的天堂，如豬肝湯、蛋黃蘿蔔糕、知高飯（豬腳飯），這裡都有。

　　與台灣相比，其他國家的夜市重點可能不是食物，實際上夜市是把一些攤販集合一起，有賣食物的像是水果、蔬菜、點心，還有玩具、衣服、影碟、飾品等，皆是以便宜或是合理的價錢販賣，常常可在夜市裡看到討價還價的畫面。如清邁最負盛名的清邁夜市，就以手工藝品及肖像畫出名，當然也有珠寶、玩具、衣服及高科技產品像是音樂光碟或是影劇光碟。雖然商品的起價與其他國家相比已經偏低了，但是你還是得跟攤商殺價才能買到最划算的商品。

　　除了世界各地的中國城外，西方社會少有夜市存在，凱恩斯夜市與美食廣場即是其中一個西方社會裡的夜市，它是澳洲第一個夜市，最初是在1991 年開始營運的戶外市場，後來近期發展成一個有 130 個攤位的室內市場，裡頭有領有酒牌的餐廳、美食街、中式按摩等等，每天夜市部分從下午五點開始營業，美食街部分則從上午 10 點一直營業到深夜，全年無休。

　　夜市不只是個可以享受美食的地方，也是個不管你在何處，特別是亞洲，可以體驗當地日常生活文化面的地方，遊客們不應該放棄這樣的探索機會。

單字片語解釋

- bazaar　*n.*　市場、市集
  There is a bazaar nearby.
  這附近有一個市場。

- poll　*n.*　投票、民意調查
  The poll reported Green Party to be leading.
  民調顯示綠黨領先。

- veritable　*adj.*　的的確確的、真實的、真正的
  It is a veritable fairyland on earth.
  那真的是個人間幻境。

- stall　*n.*　攤販、小隔間
  Most of the shops were street stalls.
  大部分商店是街頭攤販。

- ornament　*n.*　飾物、裝飾品
  You must get some ornaments for the Christmas tree.
  你一定要找些飾品來裝飾那棵聖誕樹

- handicraft　*n.*　手工藝品、手工
  Some traditional handicraft techniques are hard to maintain.
  有一些傳統手工藝品技術很難保存。

相關句型翻譯要點

1. "Taiwan, for example, is regarded as one of the world's top destinations for food lovers. It holds several famous night markets which attract food lovers to enjoy the food." 中的 for example，用來舉例說明，由它引出介紹普遍概念的例子，使用範圍用可出現在句首、句末或有時可以獨立語，插在句中並不影響句子其他部分的文法關係。另外，同樣有「如」及舉例作用的 such as 則是對複數名詞起列舉作用，文章中 "...such as fruit, vegetables, snacks, toys, clothes, movie discs and ornaments..." 譯作「…像是水果、蔬菜、點心，還有玩具、衣服、影碟、飾品等」

2. "Although the initial price is cheaper there, compared with other countries bargaining with the store keeper is needed to get the best value of the goods." 中 although「雖然…但是…」的語意要特別注意一定要翻出，所以中文譯為「雖然商品的起價與其他國家相比已經偏低了，但是你還是得跟攤商殺價才能買到最划算的商品。」

⭐ 前輩指點

　　翻譯實務工作的難處在於沒有標準答案，它並不像是其他領域的學問或是技術，有一定的程序或固定的法則去遵守，也不像回答是非題或是有固定選項的選擇題一樣，不是 YES 就是 NO，或是說一定得從 1.2.3.4 或 A.B.C.D 中選一個填上，它反而可能會是 1+B 及 NO 的綜合整合答案，並不是像在做英文科目考試中的翻譯題那樣，一個蘿蔔一個坑而有標準答案的。

　　一個蘿蔔一個坑的翻譯題情境，是設定在「考試、測驗」中，在進行實務翻譯工作時，其實不可能有這樣情境，接來的案子多半是書籍或是有相當篇幅的文件，若你做的只是按照字面一字不漏地翻出來，那產出物肯定會讓人覺得「很死」，像是機器翻譯的一樣。應該掌握的原則，是「忠於原文」，就是忠於原文要表達的意思，忠於原文產生的「意境」。不過，雖然譯者可以依不同句子、上下文、角色性格等做不同的組合表達來譯文，但並不表示譯者可以因此而加油添醋的衍生出一些原文沒有的情境或內容來替這篇文章增色。請務必記住「翻譯沒有標準答案，切忌無中生有」。

主題 **3**
觀光 3-5

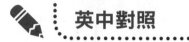

英中對照

The well-known travel guide publisher "lonely planet" used to rank ideal travel destination in the world every year. It also ranks the most accessible cities coming out in 2016 as usual. Among of them, Melbourne is not only the nearest city from Taiwan except Singapore but also the most livable city in the world. It is really worthy of visiting.

If we compare Sydney to New York in the southern hemisphere, then, Melbourne will be London in the southern hemisphere. The different temperaments of the city are revealed; it is a contrary of the classic with humanism and modern with technology. Melbourne is a city of smile. It is common to see friendly smile everywhere in the city. In addition to the famous Melbourne Cup and Australian Open, its Victorian Architecture, tram, food, fashion cloth, plays, galleries and lush gardens all make Melbourne remarkable to the world.

The mass transportation system in Melbourne leads in all direction, and this make it ranked as the most accessible city. Let's take a Melbourne visitor shuttle bus to look around attractions in the city. It costs $10 for two days; children under 10 are free. The service interval is 30 minutes. There are the following 13 stops, and all attractions around the city are included.

1. Arts Precinct
2. Federation Square
3. Sports Precinct
4. Chinatown Precinct
5. Melbourne Museum and Carlton Garden
6. Lygon Street Precinct
7. University of Melbourne
8. Queen Victoria Market
9. Harbor Town, Docklands
10. Etihad Stadium and Victoria Harbor
11. William Street
12. Southbank and Yarra River
13. The Shrine and Royal Botanic Garden

Tickets can be purchased from Melbourne Visitor Center at Federation Square or the ticket machine located at each stop. Ticket machines only accept credit cards or coins. Visitors can use the free wi-fi on the journey while listening to the audio commentary. It is a convenient and economic tourism tool.

中文

　　世人熟知的旅遊界聖經寂寞星球出版社年年皆會列出一些理想的旅遊地點評選，也如以往評論 2016 年最方便的旅遊目的地。入選地點中除了新加坡外，離台灣最近的就是墨爾本了，不僅被評選為最方便旅遊的目的地，墨爾本還是全球最適宜居住城市排名的冠軍，著實是個值得一訪的城市。

　　若說雪梨是南半球的紐約，那墨爾本就可說是南半球的倫敦，不同的城市氣質於此可見，古典人文相對於與現代摩登，各有特色。墨爾本是座微笑的城市，處處可見和善笑容，除了有名的墨爾本杯賽馬、澳網公開賽，它的維多利亞式建築、電車以及時裝、美食、戲劇、畫廊、枝稠葉茂的花園等，也讓人難以忘懷。

　　墨爾本四通八達的大眾運輸系統，更是它入選最方便旅遊目的地的主因。我們就以搭乘墨爾本觀光巴士的方式來一遊墨爾本市區景點。此巴士成人票價為兩天票澳幣 10 元，十歲以下孩童免費，每班間隔 30 分鐘，沿途有以下十三個站，涵蓋了墨爾本市所有該逛的景點。

1. 藝術特區
2. 聯邦廣場
3. 運動特區
4. 中國城區
5. 墨爾本博物館與卡爾頓花園
6. 萊貢區
7. 墨爾本大學
8. 維多利亞市場
9. 海港城、港區

10.阿提哈德體育場與維多利亞港

11.威廉街

12.南岸與亞拉河

13.神社及皇家植物園

　　車票可在聯邦廣場的遊客中心或是在每個車站的售票機購買，但售票機只能使用信用卡或是硬幣。遊客沿途可以使用免費的 wi-fi 服務聆聽語音導遊，是個便捷又經濟的觀光工具。

 **單字片語解釋**

- accessible　*adj.*　容易進入的、容易會見的
  This book is easily accessible to the young reader
  這本書很容易讓年經讀者理解。

- hemisphere　*n.*　（天體）半球
  The problems of the western hemisphere remained the same.
  西半球的問題仍未解決。

- temperament　*n.*　氣質、性情
  He reveals his own temperament.
  他洩露了自己的性情。

- lush　*adj.*　茂盛的
  He walks through a lush grassland.
  他走過一片豐盛草原。

- attraction　*n.*　景點、名勝
  Today Moon Sun Lake is a great tourist attraction.
  日月潭在今日是個絕佳旅遊景點。

- precinct　*n.*　區域、領界

  I've heard her name around the precinct.

  我已在這區久聞她的大名。

- shrine　*n.*　神社、聖地

  The meeting was held in the shrine city of Kyoto.

  會議在神社之都京都舉行。

1

翻譯技巧

2

主題範例

🔍 相關句型翻譯要點

1. "...is not only the nearest city from Taiwan except Singapore but also the most livable city in the world. It is really worthy to visit" 使用 not only... but also... 句型，帶有「不僅…而且…」意涵，所以中文譯為「**不僅**被評選為最方便旅遊的目的地外，墨爾本**還是**全球最適宜居住城市排名的冠軍…」。

2. 「**除了**有名的墨爾本杯賽馬、澳網公開賽，**它的維多利亞式建築、電車以及時裝、美食、戲劇、畫廊、枝稠葉茂的花園**等，也讓人難以忘懷。」此處為「除…以外還有…」，將後方的人／事／物「包含在內」，用於「附加說明」，使用 in addition to，而譯成為 "In addition to the famous Melbourne Cup and Australian Open, its Victorian Architecture, tram, food, fashion cloth, plays, galleries and lush gardens all make Melbourne remarkable to the world."。

⭐ 前輩指點

　　雖說在確定接案前，可能譯者早已粗略讀過原文，但在接到案子後，最先要做的首要之務還是得把原文仔細讀過一次。先全面瞭解原文，對作者所要表達的故事內容及想法才能掌握，如此進行翻譯時，也才能精準，不至於曲解作者想要表達的。一邊在細讀的同時，對反覆出現的一些關鍵字也可提高注意度，它可能在全書偏後的章節中會再度提到，或是解釋得更詳盡。在尚未正式進入譯作前，這些都可以在初始閱讀時進行準備，先記下之後該查詢的方向，收集相關資料，相信在正式開始譯書後，會比較順手及提高執行效率。

　　建議首讀時，先不要因為一時不認識的字而停頓下來去查找字典，請先一氣呵成的從頭到尾整個讀過，完整瞭解整個故事或內容後，再回過頭來查單字。有時閱讀的同時，突然有想法或是可用的字飄進腦，也該先隨手記下，留待之後正式進行翻譯時備用參考。

主題 **4**

商管 4-1

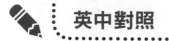

英中對照

Automobile manufacturers in the US sold seventeen million five hundred thousand sedans and light trucks in 2015, up by 5.7 % compared with sales in 2014. At the same time, the overall spending for the purchase of new car has reached to 570 billion US dollars, and the revenue for all manufacturers have reach a record high. The situation is even better than the year 2000. Small trucks and SUV were the most profitable classifications in 2015, which represented over 50% of total auto sales. The margins on these two classifications are relatively high compared with others and the average unit price has climb to $34,428. The Ford F series of small trucks and Chevrolet's Silverado and GMC Sierra from GM all achieved good sales. In the SUV classification, the compact SUV for young people in the cities, such as Honda CRV and GM Chevrolet Trax and Buick Encore, all got great sales as well.

Analysts predict the trend will continue upwards in 2016, and it will reach a peak in two years. Several positive factors, such as a low petroleum price, low interest rates and a high employment rate encourage the US population to purchase cars. On the other hand, analysts also point out the cycle of recessions after peaks which have occurred regularly through time. A recession is more likely to be severe due to recent fast developments of new types of transportation like Uber, Lyft and driverless cars. Automobiles are no longer necessities for households, and it is easy for people to utilize alternatives conveniently for travelling. The demand for cars is decreasing. It is predicted that sales might be 17.1 million units in 2016 and 15 million units entering 2019, which is the lowest point in the cycle.

中文

　　回觀 2015 年的美國汽車市場，汽車製造商總共賣出了 1,750 萬台轎車和輕型卡車，比 2014 年成長了 5.7%。同時，美國人購買新車的整體消費額達到了 570 億美元，所有製造商的利潤創了紀錄，財政情況都比 2000 年時還更好。2015 年美國汽車製造商最賺錢的車種是小卡車與越野車等大型車，銷售量超過了整體汽車業的一半以上，而且此兩種大型車銷售利潤也相對高於其他車種，將成交平均價提升到 34,428 美元。福特公司的 F 系列小卡車及通用的 Chevrolet Silverado 和 GMC Sierra 均有不錯的佳績。越野車方面，適合城市青年族群的緊湊型底盤越野車，如 Honda（本田）CRV 及通用的 Chevrolet Trax（創酷）和 Buick Encore，也都賣得不錯。

　　有分析師預估 2016 年的美國汽車市場，仍會持續看漲，達到銷售量巔峰，因為低油價、低利率和就業率等多項經濟指數都維持在正向局面，利於美國人購車，而這樣的漲勢預估會再維持 2 年。另一方面，也有分析師指出，在銷售達新高峰後，通常取之而來的就是下坡的開始。這種週期性的衰退，更有可能因近期其他新型態交通工具如 Uber、Lyft 等，及無人駕駛汽車（自動車）的快速成形，而更加劇。汽車將不再是每個家庭的必需品，人們可方便的前述其他方案取代目前的自用汽車，購車需求降低。預估美國市場 2016 年汽車銷量可能為 1710 萬輛，並在 2019 年步入 1500 萬輛的週期性低點。

單字片語解釋

- sedan　*n.*　轎車
  This car is a late-model silver sedan.
  這車是新型銀白色轎車。

- SUV 運動型多用途汽車 SUV = Sport Utility Vehicle

- compact　*adj.*　緊湊的、緊密的、小型（用於汽車）
  What do you want? Luxury, mid-size or compact?
  你要什麼車？豪華、中型還是小型車？

- margin　*n.*　邊緣、利潤、差數
  She won the seat by a margin of ten votes.
  她以十票優勢贏得席位。

- petroleum　*n.*　石油
  There is no petroleum contained in Taiwan.
  台灣沒有石油蘊藏。

- recession　*n.*　衰退、退後、不景氣
  Many businesses have closed down because of the recession.
  因經濟衰退許多企業紛紛倒閉。

相關句型翻譯要點

1. "On the other hand, analysts also point out the cycle of recessions after peaks which have occurred regularly through time." 譯文：另一方面，也有分析師指出，在銷售達新高峰後，通常取之而來的就是下坡的開始。「on the other hand 另一方面」，通常用在講同一件事情的不同面，比方在此段文字中，都在描述美國的汽車銷售情況，稍前的句子說明銷售會成長，但後面的句子雖也說明銷售量，但是重點是在描述這樣的銷售會成長但繼續往下看更久之後，是在成長至高點後進入衰退，呈現了不同的意見。

2. Ford（福特）、GM（通用）、Honda（本田）、Chevrolet Trax（創酷）等已有固定譯名，在文中第一次出現時，用圓括號引註，若之後同文中再度出現則以譯名表示即可。

3. 數值的譯文皆以阿拉伯數字表示。

⭐ 前輩指點

在進行完「細讀原文」的前置準備後，我們開始進入翻譯工作，此階段要注意的重點是將作者原文中要表達的意思，按照中文書寫習慣完整表達出來。同時也須依讀者，也就是訴求對象，選擇使用的文字。

翻譯新手第一個首要記住的要點，就是不要逐字翻譯，應該以句為單位，有時甚至以二、三句的小段落為單位，先了解原文意思翻出，再結構重組，安排一下順序，按照中文書寫習慣譯出。而字詞的使用也要依目標讀者群的習慣，使用適當的字詞。比方說原文意思為「一蹴可幾」，在譯給小朋友看時，就該化言簡意賅為淺顯易懂，改成「一下子就可以達到了」讓他們能容易理解。

建議翻譯的同時，可以做一份主要詞彙表，將用到的同一名詞或是人名稍微做個紀錄，避免同一名詞在同篇文或是同本書中使用不同譯法的錯誤發生。

主題 **4**

商管 4-2

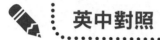

英中對照

The Chinese stock market has fallen for the second time in 7 months making people lose faith in the government's ability to regulate the market and economy.

The Shanghai Composite Index recently sank 3.5% to 2,900.97, falling 21 percent from its December high and sinking below its closing low during a $5 trillion crash in August 2015.

The decline was attributed to continual investor concerns over volatility in the yuan. The banks in Shanghai interrupted accepting shares of smaller listed companies as collateral for loans. The sell-off is a setback for the government, which battles to prevent a bad cycle of capital outflow and a weakening currency.

For Individual investors, the $5.7 trillion market is notoriously volatile. Losses in the Shanghai Composite have revealed the concerns of investors for the health of the world's second-largest economy. It's been a wild ride for Chinese investors over the past 12 months.

The market crashed over the summer as regulators failed to manage a surge in leveraged bets by individual investors after cheerleading by media enhanced the boom in mainland shares in the first half of 2014.

Even after this year's rout, the median Chinese company on mainland exchanges is valued at 55 times reported earnings, the highest level among the world's largest markets. The Shanghai Composite, which has its biggest weighting in low-priced banks and commodity companies, trades at a multiple of 15.

The Chinese currency posted the biggest weekly gain since October in Hong Kong's offshore market as the central bank limited supply of the currency and forced a narrowing of its discount to the mainland rate. Evidence of the People's Bank of China's intervention was seen on Friday in data showing the yuan dropped the most on record in December.

In equity perspective, investors ignored separate figures from the PBOC on Friday that suggested the economy could be stabilizing. Aggregate financing, China's broadest measure of new credit, rose to 1.82 trillion yuan ($276 billion) in December, compared with the median forecast of 1.15 trillion yuan in a Bloomberg survey.

The government projects that the final 2015 report will bring the full-year expansion to 6.9 percent, the slowest annual pace since 1990, and that gross domestic product growth will further slow to 6.5 percent this year.

中文

　　中國股市在七個月內第二次下跌進入熊市，再度使得人民對政府挽救管制市場及經濟能力的信心掃盡。

　　最近上海綜合指數降了 3.5% 至 2,900.97 點，與去年 12 月的高點相比，掉了百分之二十一，比 2015 年八月份 5 兆大敗收盤低點還低。

　　這消減主要歸因於長期投資人擔心人民幣過度揮發，及上海的銀行已經暫時停止接受小型公司的股票來作為貸款擔保品而來的。這樣的廉價出清可說是政府預防嚴重資金外流與趨弱幣值的一場戰爭。

　　對個別投資人而言，5.7 兆的市值蒸發及上海綜合指數的損失，已呈現了投資人對世界第二大經濟體的健全與否的擔憂。過去一年來，中國投資人可說是在經歷一場瘋狂旅程。

　　2014 年前半年大陸的股票市場在官方媒體推波助瀾下，空前繁榮，但在夏季卻因調整者疏於管理個別投資人蜂湧入市炒起的槓桿賭局，而整個崩盤。

　　但即使經過今年的大敗，中國大陸股票市場市值仍被評估為高於財報 55 倍，是世界最大市場中的最高等評比，而這上海綜合指數，對低價銀行及期貨公司有極大加權，以 15 倍數加權交易。

　　中國貨幣市場則呈現自去年十月，中央銀行管制香港離岸市場供給並縮小折扣以維持大陸利率以來最好的週營收，從週五的數據可以看出中國人民銀行的介入證據，中央銀行的人民幣 12 月時掉至最低。

1

翻譯技巧

2

主題範例

　　權證投資人大大的忽視了中國人民銀行呈現經濟平穩發展的分開的數字，與彭博調查出中值預估 1.15 兆相比，12 月的融資總額攀升至 1.82 兆人民幣（2,760 億美金）。

　　政府報告此反映出 2015 年全年的經濟成長報告擴升為 6.9%，這乃是自 1991 年開始以來，成長步調最緩慢的紀錄，預料今年的國內生產總值將會進一步下降至 6.5%。

 單字片語解釋

- volatility　*n.*　揮發性、波動性
  He discusses the management of interest rate volatility with the audience.
  他與觀眾討論利率波動的管理。

- setback　*n.*　挫折、倒退
  She met with many setbacks in the lifetime.
  她一生遭遇過很多挫折。

- surge　*n.*　洶湧、激增、大浪
  A surge of innovation in techniques is on the way.
  技術創新的浪潮即將出現。

- weighting　*n.*　權重、加值
  The tests and reports writing have equal weighting.
  考試成績與報告寫作各占一半權重。

- intervention　*n.*　介入、干預
  Her untimely intervention annoyed me.
  她不合時宜的干預惹毛我。

相關句型翻譯要點

1. "The Shanghai Composite Index recently sank 3.5% to 2,900.97, falling 21 percent from its December high and sinking below its closing low during a $5 trillion crash in August 2015." 中我們依表達方式及語言習慣的不同，譯成「最近上海綜合指數降了 3.5% 至 2,900.97 點，與去年 12 月的高點相比，掉了百分之二十一，比 2015 年八月份 5 兆大敗收盤低點還低。」句子的前後順序並不與原文相同，而是依情況調整替換，好使得文通順流暢。

2. "Even after this year's rout, the median Chinese company on mainland exchanges is valued at 55 times reported earnings, the highest level among the world's largest markets." even 在此有「已經（儘管）…卻反而…」之意涵，前面句子講股市狀況很糟，但後接的句子形容的卻是以好的狀況來點出實際是不好的，所以譯成中文時，意涵要能涵蓋到，譯成「但即使經過今年的大敗，中國大陸股票市場市值仍被評估為高於財報 55 倍」。

3. 數值、日期、百分比等，以阿拉伯數字、百分比符號表示即可。譯出文章以白話文為主，以正常速度念文章時的語氣停頓之處，作為使用標點符號逗號的位置參考。但仍需依原文來權宜決定。

⭐ 前輩指點

　　譯作進行初稿完成後，我們須自行做核對、校稿等事，把譯作與原文做核對，檢查是否有遺漏或是誤解原文意思，確保翻譯正確。除了在文字本身意涵方向上的校正外，一些為文形式上問題如錯字、贅字等也可在此檢視，一併修改。通常我們校稿時是以段落為單位，可以將自己的譯文當作是在讀一本中文書讀過，在讀的當時就可以察覺出何處不通順或是有怪怪的翻譯腔，讓人覺得不像中文，便趁此機會修改。另外，也趁此次再檢查一些固定名詞及人名的譯法，是否統一。

　　除此之外，以上基本的核對原文與校稿工作之餘，我們可再視情況加以潤飾，讓文章變得更好，比方說在固定名詞或是人名確認使用相同的以外，其他的一些曾出現過有相同語意的詞彙，可以再度檢視，使用不同的詞來表達，好過於都用同一個字，特別是在同一段落中，高頻率出現的詞彙，換其他同義字，才不會使譯文單調呆板。

　　這校稿程序，建議與初稿完成的時間有些間隔比較好，隔久一些時間再校，越容易看出問題，效果會比較好。

主題 **4**

商管 4-3

 英中對照

The majority of businesses throughout the world are family businesses, and they are the oldest and most common economic organization. The decision-making of a family business is influenced by multiple generations of a family, related by blood or marriage, who lead or own the firm. This kind of business is not always easy to study because they are not subject to financial reporting requirements, and little information is made public about financial performance. As the global economic model and the business environment changes, it has turned in a different direction toward a more open organization to maintain substantiality.

As a family member of a family business, participation as managers or owners of a business can strengthen the company; however, it might present unique problems when the dynamics of the family system and the dynamics of the business systems are not in balance. There are some good actions suggested for a family business to maintain and sustain improvements in the competitive business world.

According to researchers, successful family businesses usually take actions or operate with specific concerns which attribute to the followings,

- Separate the family and the business to build a good management system.
- Maintain the business characteristics carefully.
- Evaluate leadership candidates for the future based on the capability of the candidate and the company values.
- Adopt a serious selection process when considering the top-leaders of the organizations.

In leadership aspect, some practical family business leaders also give their advice and highlight several points for family business.

1: Parenting style should not become your leadership style - Children working in the business need to be taught and allowed to make decisions and gradually take on the responsibilities of running the business.

2: Good control ensures consistency - Good governance is essential for a family business's continuity across generations. It is dependent on balancing both legacy and renewal. Dual governance structures of an independent board and a family council are a good way to achieve this.

3: Know you're "the end" – A family business needs to have a family constitution and succession plan. Make sure it is prepared before you think you might need it.

4: Traditions, values and networks are conveyed at an early age - From a young age children are watching the current leaders make decisions that reflect the values and culture of the business. This can be a major source of competitive advantage as values, traditions and even social and business networks are transferred from one generation to the next.

5: Get an outside opinion - As the growth and complexity of the business increases, a family business tends to shift to establish a board of independent directors or to hiring non-family executives.

6: Open communication is driven from the top - This includes relationships between family members and between family members and non-family employees. Open and honest communication, a shared vision, common values, clear expectations and accountability can keep the channels of communication open.

7: Employing family - While employing family members has many advantages including a built-in desire to see the business succeed, many family businesses fall into the trap of giving their family members key positions in their business without the proper training or experience.

8: Compensating family members - Most families operate as socialists at home, but capitalists at work. This can be hard for siblings to reconcile when rewards are equally shared at home, but in the family business they are based on performance, merit and achievement.

9: Family often can't tell the difference between a big issue and a small issue - It's important for family members to have an external sounding board that allows them to step back and get some perspective.

10: Do not create two classes of employees - It is important to treat all employees equally and not favor family members over non-family members.

中文

　　世界上大多數企業為家族企業，同時，家族企業也是最古老、最常見到的經濟組織。家族企業的決策程序通常會被領導或擁有企業體的家族裡多個世代影響，他們或因血緣，或婚姻關係而有這樣的身分。家族企業不是很容易研究，因為他們並不被要求要報告財務狀況，所以財務表現很少對外界公開。隨著全球經濟模式及企業環境改變，家族企業現正轉至一個更開放的組織好能繼續維持永續經營。

　　身為家族企業中的家族成員，擔任企業中的經理或是擁有者，可以強化公司優勢，但家族系統與企業系統間的動態關係若無法平衡時，也有可能會發生特殊問題，現有一些對家族企業的行動建議提供給企業們參考，好讓這些企業可以在現今競爭激烈的企業環境裡運作維持得更好。

根據研究，成功的家族企業通常會做以下這些特別的事：
- 將家庭（族）與公司分開，建立好的管理系統。
- 小心謹慎地維持企業特徵。
- 依企業價值觀與參與人選的能力評估企業未來領導者人選。
- 採取嚴謹的評選程序來選出組織高階領導人。

一些家族企業中的實務領導人也針對領導方面，提出 10 項重點忠告如下：

1：父母教養方式不該變成領導方式—在家族企業內工作的小孩應該被教導並被允許做決策，並且漸漸地要讓他們扛上企業運作的責任。

2：好的統治管理確保連續性—良好的統治管理是家族企業能跨世代延續的基本要項，這樣的統治管理端賴於前人傳承與革新間的平衡而來，獨立董事會與家庭會議並行的雙重統治架構，對維持企業的延續性是很有作用的。

3：知道你的最後階段—家族企業需要擁有一份章程或繼承計劃，在你認為你可能需要用到前，就該先準備好。

4：傳統、價值、網絡在早期就該傳達—年紀輕的小孩該從小觀察現任領導者的決策過程，這過程通常反映了企業的價值與文化，甚至社會與商業網絡，這些代代相傳的資源，是家族企業主要的競爭優勢來源。

5：取得外部意見—企業的成長至一定程度後，由於成長與複雜性增加的關係，通常也驅使了成立獨立董事會，或是聘請非家族成員的專業經理人的需要。

6：從領導高層帶領的公開溝通—關係是家族企業成功的要件，包含了家族成員間的關係，及家族成員與非家族成員員工間的關係，公開誠摯的溝通、共享的願景、共通的價值觀、清楚的期望與職責能使得溝通管道公開。

7：雇用家人—雇用家庭成員雖有成員既定的想要此企業成功的優點存在，但是很多家族企業反而掉入了陷阱，把企業裡的重要職位給了沒有受過適當訓練或是有相關經驗的家人。

8：補償家族成員—大部分家庭在家是像社會主義者般運作，但在工作上卻是遵循資本主義；在家公平分擔，工作上卻依表現、考績與成就來賞罰，這讓手足間較難順從。

9：家族通常無法判斷發生的是大問題或是小問題—對家族企業而言，有外部傳聲筒，讓他們能後退，並得到一些看法是重要的。

10：別製造兩種不同階級員工—平等的對待所有員工是重要的，不要偏愛家族成員，更甚於非家族成員。

單字片語解釋

- governance　*n.*　統治、管理

  Corporate governance is a congregation of a series of contracts.

  公司治理是一系列契約的匯集。

- legacy　*n.*　遺產、遺贈

  Mary is the legal heir to the legacy.

  瑪莉是這分遺產的法定繼承人。

- trap　*n.*　陷阱、圈套

  They were trapped in the burning hotel.

  他們被困在發生火災的旅館裡。

🔍 相關句型翻譯要點

1. 在 "...family business, participation as managers or owners of a business can strengthen the company; however, it might present unique problems..." 中的 however 是個關係副詞，不能用來連接句子，因此需使用逗點把它從句子其他部份分開，而此處的 however 主要用來加入強調另外的點，如在此它強調了無法平衡時，反而不會有優勢，而是會產生問題。故譯作「身為家族企業中的家族成員，擔任企業中的經理或是擁有者，可以強化公司優勢，**但**若家族系統與企業系統間的動態關係若無法平衡時，也有可能會發生特殊問題…」。

⭐ 前輩指點

　　在核對原文與校稿後，即可交稿至出版社或發案主，但也許在翻譯過程中，有一些已經查過資料並請教專家仍覺得沒有把握的地方，可在交出的稿件中標示出來並加以說明解釋，請編輯進一步再度查證確認。另外有一些在翻譯進行中發現的原文資料錯誤問題，應該在譯稿中說明，也是請編輯針對有標示說明的地方再度確認，以避免錯誤。

　　交稿後仍應隨時與編輯保持聯繫，這樣若編輯對譯稿有問題時，需要及時回應，一直到書本出版上市後，才算完成案子，工作暫時算告一段落。

主題 **4**

商管 4-4

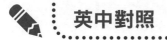

英中對照

There are several famous businessmen called "the God of Management". They hold a unique business philosophy, which is widely spread and deeply influences the business world, and is taken as the model for businessman to study and imitate.

Konosuke Matsushita was the first to be called "the god of management". He though the key to operating a business and thriving is "human" rather than the equipment. He emphasizes "human "as the essential for seeking happiness and he advocates "let human to serve humans". His catch phrase is "everyone is the chairman", which is reflected most in his business philosophy people-oriented thinking. He died in 1989, at the age of 94.

Kazuo Inamori, rescued Japan Airlines from bankruptcy and become "the god of management" even "the saint of management" after Konosuke Matsushita. He leads KDDI corporation and has operated it without a loss for 50 years. What he relies on for his successful business without being impacted by the Japanese Bubble economy is "Amoeba Management". It is operating based on the heart of people, solid philosophy, and precise divisional accounting. It divides the business into small and organized groups, amoeba, and each amoeba unit makes its own plan and manages the profit and loss by itself. Each unit grows themselves autonomously and each employee takes an active role in management. That is the outcome of "management by all", which is similar to Konosuke Matsushita's "everyone is the chairman".

The founder of Formosa Plastics Corporation, Wang Yung-Ching, who brings his business philosophy and influence to business and politics in Taiwan, is another great entrepreneur who earned "the god of management". His simple and unadorned management philosophy and quotes have been taken as an important inspirational pattern by business people, such as the following.

"Get to the bottom of things; seek the truth from facts and make everything rational."

"One dollar you earned is not yours; one dollar you saved is exactly yours."

"It takes one month to pile up the dominos, but it takes only 10 minutes to crush them all."

"It takes several decades to build up and maintain a successful business, but it might go bankrupt by only one wrong decision."

"The knack for being a successful person is to endure hardships and be capable of hard work."

Although the above emphasize different aspects in business management, which are distinctive from Japanese, they are still the model for business people to learn.

中文

商業界有不少位被稱為經營之神的名人，均有其獨樹一格的經營理念與哲學，廣為典範而流傳影響深遠，值得商業人士學習仿效。

最先有經營之神稱號的為日本松下電器的松下幸之助，他認為一個企業的壯大，並非那些軟硬體設備，關鍵應在於「人」。強調經營「初心」，是讓「人」來服務「人」，以人為本，以追求幸福為原點，他甚至有句口頭禪：「人人是總裁」，更是彰顯了他以人為本的企業經營理念。松下幸之助於1989 年離世，享壽 94 歲。

繼松下之後，幫日航破產重生的稻盛和夫，也有經營之神的稱號，甚至有人稱他「經營之聖」。稻盛領導京瓷企業 50 年沒有虧損，不受日本泡沫經濟影響，靠的就是他的「阿米巴經營」。「阿米巴經營」以人心為基礎，基於穩固的經營哲學和精緻的部門別盈虧管理，將企業劃分為「小團體」，像自由自在、重複進行細胞分裂的「阿米巴變形蟲」—以各個「阿米巴」為核心，自行制定計畫，獨立核算收支盈虧，持續自主成長，讓每位員工成為主角，實現「全員參與經營」。跟松下幸之助的「人人是總裁」有異曲同工之妙。

而台灣的經營之神，台塑企業的創辦人，王永慶，經營哲學也深深影響台灣政商界，他簡樸踏實的經營哲學及許多名言佳句更是從商者的重要精神指標。如：

「追根究底，實事求是，點點滴滴求其合理化。」
「你賺的一塊錢不是你的一塊錢，你存的一塊錢才是你的一塊錢。」
「要疊一百萬張骨牌，耗時需一個月；但倒骨牌卻只消十幾秒鐘。」
「要累積成功的企業，需耗時數十載；但要倒閉，卻只需一個錯誤的決策。」
「做人成功的秘訣在『吃必要的苦，耐必要的勞』。」

　　不同於日本的經營之神，台灣的經營之神強調的雖是不同方面的重點，但也同樣地成為成功典範，供從商者學習。

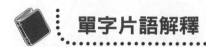

單字片語解釋

- imitate   *v.*   學習、仿效

  The little girl imitates her mother's way of singing.

  這小女孩學她媽媽唱歌的樣子。

- catch phrase 口頭禪

  That was a catch phrase he would use.

  那是他會用的口頭禪。

- amoeba   *n.*   阿米巴原蟲

  Amoeba is usually considered an animal.

  阿米巴原蟲通常被認定為動物。

- autonomously   adv.   自動地

  Robots can be controlled autonomously.

  機器人可以自動地控制。

- unadorned   *adj*.   不經修飾的、質樸的

  Her life is very simple and unadorned.

  她的生活非常簡樸。

- pile up 堆積、疊起、積累

  Work has piled up during her absence.

  工作在她離開期間堆了起來。

- domino　　*n.*　　骨牌

He touches the first domino and two days of work goes down in one minute.

他推了第一張骨牌，兩天的努力在一分鐘內倒下。

- endure　　*v.*　　耐久、忍耐

He endured three years in prison for his religious beliefs.

他為了宗教信仰在獄中忍耐吃苦三年。

🔍 相關句型翻譯要點

1. 「不同於日本的經營之神，台灣的經營之神強調的雖是不同方面的重點，但也同樣地成為成功典範，供從商者學習。」中有「雖然…但…」的語意在，翻作英文時，需要使用到 although... 譯成 "Although the above emphasize different aspects in business management, which distinctive from Japanese, they are still the model for business people to learn."

2. 「要疊一百萬張骨牌，耗時需一個月；但倒骨牌卻只消十幾秒鐘。」與「要累積成功的企業，需耗時數十載；但要倒閉，卻只需一個錯誤的決策。」兩具皆有語氣上的強烈轉折，我們使用 but 來強調，譯為 "It takes one month to pile up the dominos, but it takes only 10 minutes to crush them all." 與 "It takes several decades to build up and maintain a successful business, but it might go bankrupt by only one wrong decision."。

3. 英文的引號用於引述人物言語，而中文則以單引號表示引述人物言語。另外，分號的使用比起句號更能顯示出兩個獨立子句間的關聯性，可以依情況使用，有時中文原文中同一個段落中有數句皆是在描述同一個主詞或代名詞時，為避免使用句號造成連結性不強，可搭配用分號及結構相同的英文譯文，增強連結性。

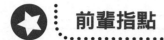

前輩指點

　　筆者曾有一段時間擔任國外中文報社編譯，當時負責翻譯的是財經與證券版面，必須將每日的原文新聞翻作中文，提供印行中文報紙給當地有中文報需求的讀者，於是乎就像跑證券新聞的記者一樣，有股票收盤新聞的時間壓力，每日中午收盤前先搜尋、選擇、翻譯財經新聞，先把除了大盤新聞外的其他新聞先處理好，接著就等收盤後進來的大盤新聞，在很短的時間內，趕緊把大盤翻譯好以趕赴印刷廠的印刷作業時間，就像在打仗一樣，非常的緊湊與刺激。不過，由於大盤新聞其實已有固定架構可用，頂多在收盤指數、分析方面依當天情勢改變內容，所以大致上都還能及時完成。

　　這種形式的翻譯雖跟書籍的翻譯不大相同，但是平日相關知識的累積功夫仍是得進行，相關股票用語、財經用語也得累積，而且也應多多參考同業對相關新聞的翻譯用語，學著用並且要能熟悉，每日遇到不同的收盤情況時，才得以派上用場，不開天窗。

主題 4
商管 4-5

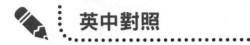

英中對照

Triangular trade is one account of the GDP (gross national product), and it is a business model that takes orders in Taiwan then manufacturers the commodities overseas. It has gradually become a major income towards GDP since 2001. For example, Foxconn Technology Group takes orders from Apple in Taiwan, and it manufactures the products for the order in its China factory. The income for Taiwan is the difference of the total amount of the orders minus manufacturing costs in China, which represents the additional value of Taiwan's research and development, marketing, and administration. It is a sort of exported service, and it also represents the biggest portion of Taiwan's service export sector.

The triangular trade income breaks through 20 billion US dollars to 20.8 billion US dollars for the first time in 2014, which is converted to 631.6 billion new Taiwan dollars. It contributes to GDP more than inbound tourism income, which adds up to 14.6 billion US dollars. According to the research of CIER (Chung-Hua Institution for Economic Research), it shows the risk of supply chain disruption. As the percentage of overseas manufacturing becomes higher and higher; the need for supply chain localization in China is increasing. As the local supply chain is increasing in China, the percentage of exported intermediate goods from Taiwan to China is decreasing. There will be impacts on the export sector in Taiwan. Taiwan's triangular income and numbers of orders decrease, and the model might change to "take the orders in China, and manufacture the orders in China".

Due to the risk of disruption, CIER has urged two solutions to solve the problem. They are "to search for new overseas manufacturing bases" and "make alliances with minor foes to fight against the major enemy". The government should consider adjusting settings on financial rules and pricing based on changes in the overall business environment. By doing so, the overseas manufacturing base becomes another source of income so that the opportunity can be created for Taiwan to advance its technology and develop products. To take Taiwan as the R&D center, and take the overseas base as the manufacturing center. No matter what size the base is, there is no harm for Taiwan.

As the "Red supply chain" is raised, the local brands in mainland China grow, too. Chinese brands have started to snatch the market share of existing Japanese and Korean brands. The situation between Taiwan and China has changed from vertical specialization to horizontal competition. A new development plan should be taken to step up to the next level. It is recommended to cooperate with international brands, for example, to form alliance with minor foes like Japan and Korea to fight against China on the Internet of Things (IOT) in order to eliminate the risk.

中文

　　三角貿易是國民所得帳中的項目，是一種在台灣接單、海外生產的商業模式，是在 2001 年成形後才有的所得項目。例如鴻海接了蘋果的訂單，交給中國大陸的廠生產，接單金額減去付給大陸的加工費，剩下的就是在台灣的三角貿易收入。這收入就是台灣的管銷、研發所創造的附加價值。三角貿易屬於服務輸出，目前是台灣最大的服務輸出項目。

　　2014 年台灣的三角貿易收入首度突破 200 億美元，達 208 億美元，合新台幣 6,316 億元。同年外人來台旅行收入是 146 億美元，三角貿易對國內生產毛額 (GDP) 的貢獻比外人來台旅行還高。但是根據中經院的研究報告顯示，台灣的三角貿易出現「斷鏈」危機。由於海外生產比例愈來愈高，衍生供應鏈在地化需求，大陸供應鏈崛起，大陸從台灣進口「中間財」的比重在下降中，造成台灣接單減少、三角貿易收入縮小，衝擊了中間財的出口，未來可能變成「大陸接單、大陸生產」。

　　針對此斷鏈危機，中經院提出了「重新尋覓海外生產基地」和「聯合次要敵人打擊主要敵人」兩對策來解決危機。政府的財稅法規與廠商訂價，應思索如何配合整個環境變遷而重新分配，將海外生產基地變成另一個利潤來源，如此才能創造台灣本土進行更多技術升級與產品發展的機會。讓台灣本地為研發中心，海外為生產中心。海外基地再大，對台灣也沒壞處。

　　而面對大陸紅色供應鏈崛起，兩岸從垂直分工變成水平競爭，大陸本土品牌也興起，掠奪了原本日本品牌、南韓品牌的市場，台廠應試著與國際品牌大廠合作跨入新領域，聯合日、韓次要敵人來打擊主要敵人大陸，例如台日、台韓合攻物聯網時代商機，來解決危機。

單字片語解釋

- triangular　*adj.*　三角的、三角形的
  The scapula is a triangular bone.
  肩頰骨是一塊三角形的骨頭。

- GDP (gross national income) 國民生產毛額

- convert　*v.*　兌換、轉變
  These machines convert cotton into cloth.
  這些機器將棉花轉換成布料。

- disruption　*n.*　中斷、瓦解
  The country was in disruption.
  國家處在分裂中。

- alliance　*n.*　聯盟
  They made an alliance against the common enemy.
  它們結盟來對抗共同敵人。

- the Internet of Things (IOT) 物聯網

Q 相關句型翻譯要點

1. 首段中主詞三角貿易翻作英文時，可用 it 來代替，避免相同字詞重複出現太多次。如 "Triangular trade is one account of the GDP (gross national product), and it is a business model that takes orders in Taiwan then manufacturers the commodities overseas. It has gradually become a major income towards GDP since 2001."

2. 涉及金額時，中文英文表示方法不同，要以阿拉伯數字合併金額單位來表示，如文中原中文以 200 億美元表示，翻作英文時，則須改為 20 billion US dollars，而原中文新台幣 6,316 億元譯成英文表示時，就得轉換為 631.6 billion new Taiwan dollars，此應特別注意。

前輩指點

　　接翻譯案子，進行進度的掌控，是相當重要的一環，特別是接的若是整本書籍的翻譯，時間進度的掌控，更是一大挑戰。接案之初，編輯應會與你討論進度與交稿方式，約定大致時間表，建議新手自己在執行時，要以比編輯還更超前一點的進度來進行，好有空間與彈性來調整及跟進進度，因為在翻譯進行當中，還不知道會臨時出現什麼狀況，耽擱了譯書的進行，特別是新手不見得是全職譯者，原本正職事務上不巧突然有意外，工作被打斷，能擠出的其他時間有限，阻礙外接譯案的進度。

　　建議譯者對自己要嚴格一點，督促自己嚴謹進行「今日事今日畢」原則，每天一定要做到原先自己預定的進度，比方說一天譯一個章節或是譯某個字數。最好自己的進度還要能比編輯或發案方的進度還超前，這樣若有突發狀況發生，至少調整的空間比較大，減少開天窗的機會。平日生活也最好盡量維持理想，隨時保持精神狀態的平穩，因為翻譯是一項花腦力的工作，精神狀態不佳時，是無法做好這份工作，維持理想的譯文水準的。

主題 5
歷史 5-1

 英中對照

There are several female emperors in western history, and Mary I of Scotland is the most famous one among the emperors of Scotland. She is not well-known for excellent political achievements like Elizabeth I, Queen of England who ended her life, but noted for her unfortunate life with three marriages.

Mary Stuart was born in 1542. Her father James V died 6 days after her birth. It is said James V sighed "It comes with a lass; it will pass with a lass!" upon hearing of the birth of Mary before he died. His ruefully exclamation partially came true like it was meant to be. Mary I was the last monarch of the House of Stewart in Scotland.

Mary was crowned in Stirling Castle when she was 9 months old and she was sent to France by her French mother, Marie de Guise. She was protected by political marriage with France, and she married the Dauphin of France, Francis, when she was 15 years old in 1558. Her husband was crowned as King François II making Mary queen consort of France after the French King, Henry II passed away in 1559. The young French king, however, died from disease a year after the marriage. Mary became a widow at 17.

Mary returned to Scotland after her husband's death. In order to consolidate the throne, she married her cousin, Henry Stewart, Lord Darnley, who held royal lineage in both England and Scotland. Darnley was killed in an explosion only few months after Mary gave birth to her son, James, in 1566. There was a rumor about Mary murdering her husband on purpose. Although the rumors disadvantaged Mary, she consented to marry James Hepburn, Earl of Bothwell, only three months later. This marriage made Mary lose her reputation. Her subjects took her as a whore and waged forces against her. Mary was compelled to abdicate the throne in favor of her 1 year old infant son.

In 1568, Mary escaped to England asking her cousin, Elizabeth, for help. Elizabeth I imprisoned Mary for 18 years instead of helping her due to her scruple about Mary being eligible to take the throne of England. In 1587, Mary, at the age of 44, was executed for treason by Elizabeth's order for plotting to assassinate Elizabeth. The unmarried Elizabeth without heirs demised the throne to Mary's son, James VI of Scotland and James I of England when she died in1603. James became the first king of the Union of the Crowns. In 1612, James moved his mother's body to Westminster Abbey and reinterred it in a chapel next to her ancestor, Henry VII and opposite the tomb of Elizabeth I's. Mary's unfortunate life makes people sigh throughout time, and has become the sources of writing themes. Mary has become the most famous of Scotland's monarchs.

中文

　　西洋史中有不少位女性君主存在，瑪莉女王是蘇格蘭君主中名氣最大的，之所以有名，不是因為她政績卓越，與終結她生命的英格蘭女王伊莉莎白一世相比，反倒是因為她擁有三段婚姻的多舛人生。

　　瑪莉・斯圖爾特生於西元 1542 年，才出生六天父親詹姆士五世（James V）便過世了，據說詹姆士五世臨終前得知女兒出生消息時，感慨著說著：「它隨著姑娘來，亦隨著姑娘去」。這話似乎在冥冥中被部分應驗，瑪莉一世女王是蘇格蘭斯圖爾特王朝最後一位君王。

　　瑪莉九個月大時便在史特靈城堡（Stirling Castle）加冕為女王，在法籍母親吉斯的瑪麗（Marie de Guise）安排下被送回法國，透過政治聯姻手段受到法國的保護。1558 年，瑪莉十五歲時嫁給法國皇太子，1559 年，法王亨利二世病逝，她丈夫登基成為法王法蘭索瓦二世（François II），她也加冕為法國皇后。但年輕的法王在與瑪莉結婚後一年也病逝，瑪莉 17 歲就成了寡婦。

　　瑪莉回到故鄉蘇格蘭，為了鞏固王權，她嫁給了同時具有英格蘭與蘇格蘭血統的表親—達恩利勳爵，亨利・斯圖亞特（Henry Stuart, Lord Darnley）。但在 1566 年，瑪莉在愛丁堡城堡生下兒子詹姆士後不久，達恩利勳爵便在一次爆炸中身亡。有傳言說達恩利是被瑪莉謀殺的，儘管流言對瑪莉不利，她卻在三個月後，同意嫁給了伯斯維爾伯爵四世，詹姆士・赫伯恩（James Hepburn）。這一嫁更讓她威望大失，臣民視她為淫婦，紛紛起兵反叛，在不得已的情況下，她被迫讓位給僅有一歲大的兒子。

　　1568 年，瑪莉逃往英格蘭，向表親英格蘭女王伊莉莎白一世求助，伊莉莎白卻因為瑪莉具有繼承英格蘭王位的血統而有所顧忌，反而把瑪莉囚禁起來，一關就是十八年。1587 年，伊莉莎白以瑪莉密謀殺害她為由，下令處決了 44 歲的瑪莉。1603 年，伊莉莎白一世病逝，一生未婚無子嗣的她將王位傳給瑪莉的兒子，他是英格蘭國王詹姆士一世，亦是蘇格蘭國王詹姆士六世，成為共主聯邦（Union of the Crowns）的第一任國王。1612 年時，詹姆士六世將母親遺體移至西敏寺安葬，墓穴就隔著先祖亨利七世與伊莉莎白一世對望，還真令人唏噓感嘆。瑪莉女王一生命允多舛，使她成為後人書寫題材，也成了蘇格蘭最為眾人所知的君主。

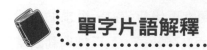 **單字片語解釋**

- emperor　*n.*　皇帝、君主

  The emperor lavished the general gifts.

  皇帝賞賜將軍豐厚禮物。

- monarch　*n.*　君主

  The monarch was ousted by a military coup.

  那位君主被軍事政變者廢黜了。

- throne　*n.*　王位、王權、寶座

  He renounced his claim to the French throne.

  他正式放棄法國王位繼承權。

- subject　*n.*　臣民、國民

  The Queen is supposed to be responsible for her subjects.

  女王照理應該對她的臣民們負責。

- abdicate　*v.*　退位、放棄

  The old king must abdicate to the new.

  老國王應該讓位給新國王

- treason　*n.*　叛國罪、謀反

  He was executed for treason.

  他因叛國罪被處死刑。

- assassinate　*v.*　暗殺、中傷

The police exposed a criminal plot to assassinate the president.

警方偵破了暗殺總統的陰謀

- demise　*v.*　讓位

He demised to his son.

他讓位給他的兒子。

🔍 相關句型翻譯要點

1. 年分、數字、數值僅以阿拉伯數字譯出即可。

2. 英語語法有時態、詞性變化，中翻英時必須看完整個句子、段落後，了解意思後譯出，每個句子皆須選擇文法及時態，此單元為歷史相關人物，已發生的事實多半使用到過去式。另外，部分動詞須以被動式使用，也須注意並搭配使用。

3. 專有名詞的人名，需先查證固有譯名，若無固有譯名，則應以羅馬拼音譯出，並在括號內附上原文，而本單元文中人名原皆為英文名，故直接譯回原文，不需附上中文譯文。

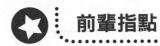

前輩指點

　　本單元歷史主題類的文章，特別是偏向歷史相關人物描述的，多半不會有太複雜的文法或句型，大部分是敘事性的描述或是故事情節。不管是中翻英或是英翻中，比較需要注意的便是特定詞及相對應的時勢邏輯。

　　有些翻譯者選擇專攻某一領域文章，朝特定專業範疇邁進，翻來便得心應手，不需花費多時，因為他平時可能就已有大量專精範圍的背景知識做為根基，長期浸濡其中，翻譯此特定範疇主題或類型，自然更易達成最佳化的翻譯工作進行模式。

　　而部分譯者可能因為進場時間先後的問題，尚無法擇一專攻領域，就只能先以「廣」來逐漸建立其翻譯形象，因此有可能遇到各式各樣主題。這時候，假裝自己是某特定領域的老師，如同編制講義般的教導著學生不失為一靈活變通的方法。比方說原本對歷史沒特別興趣的譯者，在翻譯歷史相關文章時，就可以試著逼自己當起歷史老師，像老師般的講故事給學生聽。

主題 5
歷史 5-2

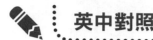

英中對照

St. Joan of Arc, 1412 to 1431, nicknamed the Maid of Orleans, is a very famous saint in France. She hindered the English army from occupying France during the Hundred Year's war, and she became known as the Fortune, the protector God of France.

Joan of Arc grew up in the rural area of Doeremy, and she went to church and confessed to the priest very often since she is young. It is said she could see anomalies especially images related to saints. Joan of Arc decided to devote herself to the army when she was 16 years old, and she disguised herself with a male appearance. She went to the palace through a special channel to present the "call" from God to the uncrowned king Charles VII. The "call" resulted in her leading the French force to save Orleans and assisted the king to retain the throne of France. Joan of Arc, a farm girl without professional military training and education, like a missionary, completed the task assigned from God by waving a flag with the figure of Christ and his two angles in the battlefield and writing the declaration of the war to send to English occupied territory. She won the war spiritually and recovered Orleans.

Charles VII did not want to be involved in the war anymore after his coronation; however, Joan of Arc thought the recovery task should continue as long as there were still English people occupying French territory. The king conferred nobility on her and assigned small tasks to her. She steadily lost battles and there were hundreds of people who left her army in the end. She was finally imprisoned in a castle of Rouen. The church set her up as a herestic and handed her to the English army. Joan of Arc was sentenced to death by burning at the stake at the hands of the English force.

St. Joan of Arc's death was a grievance for five hundred years. She was not beatified and canonized by the Vatican until five hundred years later. These titles, that people granted her when reminiscing about her kind-hearted and honesty from the 16th century to the 19th century, can be taken as long-awaited justice for sure.

中文

　　聖女貞德（1412-1431），是法國史上非常有名的聖徒，她在英法百年戰爭（Hundred Years' War）中，阻止了英軍佔領法國，因而以「幸運之神」聞名，又為法國的守護神。

　　貞德生長在東雷米的鄉下地方，自小常上教堂做禮拜、向神父告解，據說貞德少時就能看到異相，特別是有關聖者的畫面。十六歲時她決定投身於軍隊，喬裝成男子透過管道到殿堂上向未登基的國王查理七世講述她聽到的「召喚」，這召喚軀使她獲准指揮為解救奧爾良而徵集的軍隊，並輔助國王登上法國君主寶座。從未受過軍事訓練及太多正規教育的村姑貞德，特別帶著一面有基督像及兩位天使的軍旗上戰場，還手寫宣言派送去英國人的地盤，她施展神跡似的擊退了英國人，收回了奧爾良，讓查理七世順利登基。

　　登基後的查理七世，不想再打仗，但貞德則認為法國土地上仍有英國人，應該要繼續收復的任務，於是國王冊封貞德為貴族，只派任一些小任務讓她去完成，後來她帶領的軍隊只剩幾百人，節節敗退後她被關在盧昂（Rouen）的一個城堡中，反被教會誣害指為異端。教會把她交給英軍，英軍將她活活燒死。

　　貞德含冤而死，一直到五百年後，梵蒂岡教廷才為貞德平反，將她冊封為聖女貞德，平復五百年來的冤屈。從十六世紀到十九世紀以來，世人為了懷念她的善良、正直而給的諸多封號，也可算是遲來的正義了。

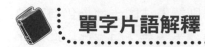

單字片語解釋

- maid   *n.*   少女、女僕
  They had a cook and a maid.
  他們有一位廚師及女僕。

- saint   *n.*   聖徒、聖人
  She was made a saint.
  她被封為聖人。

- hinder   *v.*   阻止、牽制
  Heavy snow hindered the construction work.
  大雪阻礙了建築工程的進度。

- throne   *n.*   王座、帝位
  The King's eldest son is the heir to the throne.
  國王的長子是王位繼承人。

- confer   *v.*   授與、協商
  She will confer with him on the subject.
  她將與他討論此問題。

- heretic　　*n.*　　異端、異教

  She was burned at the stake for heretic.

  她因異端邪說而被處火刑至死。

- grant　　*v.*　　授予、承認

  They may grant you power, honor, and riches

  他們可能會給予你權力、榮耀與財富。

- reminisce　　*v.*　　緬懷、追憶

  Reminiscing makes me feel old.

  追憶使我感到老了。

🔍 相關句型翻譯要點

1. 「登基後的查理七世，不想再打仗，但貞德則認為法國土地上仍有英國人，應該要繼續收復的任務。」句中的但有轉折語氣，因此我們翻成英文時，使用 **however** 來強調此轉折語氣 "Charles VII did not want to be involved in the war anymore after his coronation; **however**, Joan of Arc thought the recovery task should continue... occupying French territory."

2. 年分、數字、數值僅以阿拉伯數字譯出即可。

3. 英語語法有時態、詞性變化，中翻英時必須看完整個句子、段落後，了解意思後譯出，每個句子皆須選擇文法及時態，此單元為歷史相關人物，已發生的事實多半使用到過去式。另外，部分動詞須以被動式使用，也須注意並搭配使用。

4. 專有名詞的人名，需先查證固有譯名，若無固有譯名，則應以羅馬拼音譯出，並在括號內附上原文，而本單元文中人名原皆為英文名，故直接譯回原文，不需附上中文譯文。

⭐ 前輩指點

　　西洋史相關範疇，有非常大的機會會與宗教範圍重疊，在翻譯此類文章時，本身若非基督教或是天主教徒背景，就得先花上一些時間，給自己先補充一下相關知識，避免誤譯發生。

　　倒是沒有必要一定得把當時那段時間發生的事讀到滾瓜爛熟，才來開始進行翻譯工作，但有些基本認識與了解是必要的。自己得善加安排時間，也別讀著讀著忘了「翻譯正事」，影響到進度。

　　本篇為例，仍是偏重在描述貞德故事的文章，句型簡單，變化不大。但請務必確認內容詳實正確。當然，原先就屬謠言或是「據說」的部分，真實性我們就無從考究也不需去考究，僅恰如其分地將原文譯出即可。

主題 5
歷史 5-3

 英中對照

Qin Shi Huang, the first king who used Emperor as his title throughout Chinese history, was born in the city of Handan, Zhao in 259 BC. He was the son of King Zhaoxiang of Qin, named Ying Zheng and also known as Zhou Zheng. He was crowned at the age of 13. Qin Shi Huang built up the Qing dynasty by unifying all warring states as one China at his age of 39, and he reigned over the country for 37 years.

This "unrepeatable" emperor indeed initiated many constructive and influential measures such as unifying Chinese scripts, standardizing the currency and the units of measurements. He facilitated the transport system by making the axles of carts all the same lengths. He constructed Lingqu canal and the Great wall. In administrative aspects, he implemented centralization in the administrative system and completely abolished feudalism. The whole of China was divided into several levels of administrative units such as commanderies and counties.

Qin Shi Huang; however, did behaved controversially in some aspects, like burning books and burying scholars alive. He also implemented strict laws and harsh punishments on people. He gave himself up to pleasure by levying heavily taxes on people and spent it on seeking the elixir of life, building luxury palaces, etc.

There are statements about the formation of his specific character. It is said his specific character comes from his birth and family background. Although he was officially the son of King Zhaoxiang of Qin and Zhao Ji, Lu Buwei's concubine, it is said he was actually the son of Lu Buwei. Lu Buwei initially presented the pregnant Zhao Ji to King Zhaoxiang of Qin with political intentions, but this is still an unknown myth. He spent his childhood like an abandoned child without a mother in the state of Zhou before he was eight and he bore bullying and humiliation until then. This experience harmed his mind and sowed the seeds of his extreme personality. He even did not hold the actual power at the beginning when he became the king of Qin. He was just a puppet that Lu Buwei played and controlled at that time. On the other hand, his promiscuous queen mother and relatives like Lao Ai's attempted a coup to disadvantage his reign. He was forced to eliminate the sources of chaos with extremely cruel methods until he gradually became mature and rock-solid on the throne.

No matter what the truth is about his birth and the background of Qin Shi Huang, it has all become a part of history, buried in the ground after his death during the fifth perambulatory tour in 210 BC.

中文

　　中國歷史上第一位使用「皇帝」稱號的君主秦始皇，於公元前 259 年出生於趙國的邯鄲，他是秦莊襄王的兒子，名為嬴政，又稱趙政，13 歲時登上王位，39 歲統一中國，建立秦朝，在位 37 年。

　　這一位「空前」的皇帝，的確開啟了許多具建設性並影響日後中國深遠的措施，如統一文字、貨幣及度量衡；他建立了車同軌、道同距的交通系統，並修建靈渠及萬里長城；行政方面，他實行中央集權制度，廢分封及立郡縣，全中國被劃分成許多不同的地方行政層級，像是郡、縣。

　　然而，秦始皇同時也有其他不少負面作為引人爭議，如焚書坑儒。他同時也實施嚴刑峻法。他向人民課重稅，以供給自身奢侈的生活，並追求永生、修建宮室。

　　有一些針對他特殊人格形成的說法流傳著，包括身世之謎及成長背景。雖然名義上他是秦莊襄王與呂不韋的姬妾趙氏所生的兒子，但有傳聞說他其實是呂不韋之子，呂不韋當初是出於政治目的，將已經懷上他骨肉的趙姬獻給秦莊襄王，一直到現在這仍是個未解之謎。在他八歲前，他像是被母親遺棄般，被丟在趙國不管，並受盡了欺侮、羞辱；據知這段宛如「棄子」的生活，帶給他心靈傷害，日後的極端性格應就是於此時埋下的種子。甚至在他即位時，他僅有君王之名，無君王之實；只能當呂不韋的傀儡。另一方面，母后的淫亂及其他相關對他不利的情勢如嫪毐之亂，更逼他不得不在實力壯大時，以殘酷手段一次解決亂源。

　　不管關於秦始皇的身世及成長背景的真相如何，都在西元前 210 年，他第五度巡行天下途中病死後，一同埋進土裡，成為歷史的一部分了。

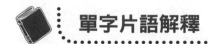

單字片語解釋

- unify *v.* 統一
  The new leader hopes to unify the country.
  新領導者希望把國家統一起來。

- abolish *v.* 廢除、撤銷
  She plans to abolish the monarchy.
  她計畫廢除君主專政。

- feudalism *n.* 封建制度、封建主義
  By 1740 European feudalism was in its death throes.
  時至 1740 年，歐洲的封建主義已搖搖欲墜。

- commandery *n.* 騎士團管理地、會所、郡
  Commandery is an historical administrative level of China
  郡是中國歷史上的一種行政管理單位。

- levy *v.* 徵稅、索取、收集
  The local government levy a tax on him.
  地方政府向他徵稅。

- elixir　*n.*　長生不老藥、煉丹術

  Is there any possibility to get an elixir?

  有可能找得到長生不老藥嗎？

- sow　*v.*　散布、播種

  It is too soon to sow yet.

  現在還不是播種的時機。

🔍 相關句型翻譯要點

1. 「雖然名義上他是秦庄襄王與呂不韋的姬妾趙氏所生的兒子，但有傳聞說他其實是呂不韋之子」我們使用 Although..., 句型來譯出 "**Although** he was officially the son of King Zhaoxiang of Qin and Zhao Ji, Lu Buwei's concubine, it is said he was actually the son of Lu Buwei." **although 不能放句尾，也不可以與 but 同時使用。**

2. 「不管關於秦始皇的身世及成長背景的真相如何，」我們使用 no matter what... 的句型來譯出 "No matter what the truth is about his birth and the background of Qin Shi Huang"。

★ 前輩指點

　　開始嘗試擔任自由譯者，其實是個需要勇氣的決定，通常一開始時，大部分譯者應該都不是以專職譯者身分在接案，除非是經濟狀況暫無憂虞，仍有一筆為數可觀的生活費可運用。一般常見情形是以兼職的方式接案，本身通常都還有正職工作。因為不管是翻譯社或出版社，稿費都不會是固定穩定的每月進你的銀行帳戶，對於自己收入現金流的規劃，最好能好好掌握，免得斷炊喝西北風。

　　不要因為對「睡到自然醒」的美好想像而投入自由譯者工作，對過度地帶前的譯者而言，在正職工作外還要多安排出此兼職工作的時間與精力，不見得會那麼美好的如你所願。反倒有可能身體搞差了，錢也沒多賺多少，不過，沒有實際實行，親身體會，當然也永遠不知可行不可行。

　　文字工作者，精神壓力大過於生理壓力，但是若身體狀況也不是很穩定健康的話，精神亦很難能支撐趕稿與額外工作時間，因此真的得要好好評估後再行動才是。

主題 5
歷史 5-4

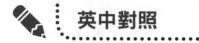 英中對照

Adolf Hitler, the No. 1 war criminal of World War II, was born on 20thApril, 1889 in Austria. He was not only a famous politician, but also an ambitious military leader who sought for aggressive expansion. He rose to power rapidly after joining the National Socialist German Workers Party, which was also known as the Nazi Party in 1919. He transformed the Democratic Republic of Germany into the totalitarian dictatorship Germany after he became the chancellor of Germany in 1933. He initiated World War II by invading Poland in 1939, and occupied most of Europe, North Africa, East Asia and Asia Pacific regions with Axis countries Japan and Italy. After 1942, the Allies started to fight back and turn the war around. Germany was going down gradually and losing the war. Hitler finally committed suicide with newlywed wife, Eva Braun, on April 30, 1945 when the Soviets army advanced on Berlin.

There are several hearsays for the death of this controversial person. It is said he escaped to South America planning to bounce back. There is also a saying he became a shepherd and spent the rest of his life in the Alps. Some other rumors about his private life allow people to get more understanding about him.

Hitler, a slaughterer who took millions of lives, was a vegetarian. He did not drink coffee, strong tea or white wine. He thought meat, alcohol and nicotine were harmful to the human body. Hitler did not specifically pay attention to material life. He did not like to wear a tuxedo or spend time on knotting a tie. He wore a cap with a big brim all the time to protect eyes from the sun. He did not like sunshine. He hated all holidays and he prohibited singing songs for thanksgiving and lighting up candles on Christmas trees. Hitler was a very emotional person. He tended to be cool and cruel with a careless attitude to everything one day but talkative and energized in high spirits the next. The only entertainment that he enjoyed was magic-trick performances. Although he laughed when he saw funny shows, it is rare to see him laughs aloud.

On the other hand, people are suspicious of Hitler's sexual orientation. A German historian, Lothar Machtan asserted that Hitler was a homosexual and he hid the truth of the conflict between his sexual orientation and enthusiasm for the pursuit of power. Historians, who studied relevant evidence, found he never had a smooth relationship with women and he expressed obvious passion and sexual excitement to men. It has also been found that he had several homoerotic friendships at an earlier age. Although there were 15,000 homosexuals tortured and sent to concentration camps due to the stringent law in Nazi Germany, Hitler himself never spoke about that publicly.

People who hold extremely unique personalities usually achieve something extremely unique. Adolf Hitler indeed is one example among them.

中文

　　第二次世界大戰頭號戰犯希特勒，於 1889 年 4 月 20 日出生於奧地利，他不僅是個舉世聞名的政治人物，也是位野心勃勃積極擴張的軍事家。他在 1919 年時加入了德國工人黨（後來的納粹黨）後快速竄升，在 1933 年成為德國總理後，便將德國從民主共和轉為納粹一黨專政的極權獨裁國家。更在 1939 年時入侵波蘭，開啟第二次世界大戰，與日本、義大利等軸心國佔領了大部分歐洲、北非、東亞及太平洋區域。在 1942 年後，同盟國開始反攻，德軍漸趨劣勢，最後希特勒在蘇聯紅軍逼近柏林時，與剛結婚的女友愛娃‧布勞恩在 1945 年 4 月 30 日自殺結束了生命。

　　這位極具爭議性人物的死，也具爭議的有諸多說法，有人說他其實沒死，逃到了南美圖謀東山再起，也有人說他成了阿爾卑斯山上的牧羊人，就此終老。除了死亡實情眾說紛紜外，他生前的私人生活，也有一些小道消息流傳，使世人得以一窺全貌。

　　這位屠殺人無數的希特勒，是位素食主義者，他不喝咖啡、濃茶及白酒，認為肉食、酒精、尼古丁對人體有害，而他不是特別重視物質生活，不喜歡穿燕尾服，也不喜歡花時間打領帶，他不時地戴著大帽檐軍帽，據說是為了要保護眼睛不受陽光刺激，他不喜歡陽光。他討厭大部分節日，禁止人唱感恩歌，禁止點燃聖誕樹上的蠟燭。希特勒是個相當情緒化的人，可能前一天超級冷漠，對任何事都不關心，隔天就完全相反精神抖擻地滔滔不絕，神采飛揚。他唯一的休閒娛樂，應該就是欣賞魔術表演，但據說看到有趣表演時，他雖然會笑，但仍很少見到他放聲爽朗大笑。

　　另外，世人對於希特勒的性向，也有頗多猜測，一位德國的歷史學家馬赫丹就斷定希特勒是同性戀，他之所以隱瞞事實是因為他的性向與他對權利的狂熱追求產生了衝突。歷史學家發現他和女人的關係從沒有圓滿過。有其他相關證據顯示了希特勒對男人的激情與明顯的性亢奮，他在早期更有數段有同性愛性質的友誼關係，而納粹德國時代，執行嚴苛法律，有 1.5 萬同性戀者因此被送入集中營，遭到迫害，但希特勒本人卻從未對同性戀公開發表過任何評論。

　　具有極端人格的人，常有不同於一般人的成就及作為，希特勒即是一例。

單字片語解釋

- totalitarian　*adj.*　集權主義的、極權主義者
  Some totalitarian states impose embracive controls
  一些集權主義國家實施全面控制。

- dictatorship　*n.*　獨裁政權
  A dictatorship is usually an efficient government.
  獨裁政權通常會是個有效率的政府。

- Axis　*n.*　二次世界大戰時的軸心國

- Allies　*n.*　二次世界大戰時的同盟國

- hearsay　*n.*　傳聞
  I knew by hearsays that he was the reporter of the Times.
  我聽說他是時代雜誌的記者。

- slaughterer　*n.*　屠殺、劊子手、屠殺者
  He had no strong feelings about the slaughter.
  他對那場屠殺沒有感覺。

- homoerotic　*adj.*　同性戀（愛）的

  His early works included a lot of homoerotic scenes.

  他早期作品包含很多同性戀場景。

- concentration camp 集中營

  He was caught and sent to a Nazi concentration camp.

  他被抓起來，送往納粹集中營。

1

翻譯技巧

2

主題範例

相關句型翻譯要點

1. 中文「…他不僅是個舉世聞名的政治人物，也是位野心勃勃積極擴張的軍事家。」有「不僅／不但…而且…」的涵意在，所以我們使用 not only...but (also) 句型來譯出 "He was not only a famous politician, but also an ambitious military leader who sought for aggressive expansion." 此為對等連接詞，所連接的兩個單字，須為相同詞性。

2. 使用分號來連接獨立子句，比使用句號更能顯示出兩個子句間的關聯性。如："After 1942, the Allies started to fight back and turn the war around. Germany was going down gradually and losing the war." 及 "Hitler did not specifically pay attention to material life. He did not like to wear a tuxedo or spend time on knotting a tie."

3. 我們使用 Although..., 句型來譯出 "Although there were 15,000 homosexuals tortured and sent to concentration camps due to the stringent law in Nazi Germany, Hitler himself never spoke about that publicly." although 不能放句尾，也不可以與 but 同時使用。

4. 年分、數字、數值僅以阿拉伯數字譯出即可。

★ 前輩指點

　　不同類型的翻譯案子中，有部分是相對比較能成為穩定收入來源的，比方說公司行號、字幕翻譯等。另外，專業類別的翻譯，如商業金融類通常報酬行情相對稍微好一些，但通常要求的完成時間都較短，時間上比較緊迫。建議譯者接案時，在比例安排上，可先排些基本的會有固定進帳的案子，之後多出來的再排些本身興趣考量，而稿酬不見得相對應的案子。先求溫飽再進而考慮興趣及想專攻的方向。

　　同時對於自己接的案子，該建立個管控表格或是紀錄工具，因為每個案子的進帳時間往往依不同業主而有不同，特別是一般企業客戶，付款時間都不一定，若自己沒個整理記錄，到時可能沒領到稿酬都不知道，做了白工。建議可運用 excel 定期記錄每筆接下的案子，及相對的稿酬收付狀況，自行做好簡單收支管理。

主題 **6**

教育 6-1

 英中對照

It is common that Asian parents keep "the perception of winning" as the starting point and they also get the idea that by 3 years life is set. Most Asian parents pay high attention to pre-school education or start providing a formal learning for their children earlier. They expect their kids to get better achievement in the future because of earlier learning and brain development.

Parents in western countries with great intellectual achievement are found to adopt different methods that are contrary to eastern countries. The western preschool education practice is worthy to be taken as the reference to improve preschool education in Asia.

For example, pre-schools (Vorschule) were abolished in the constitutional rule (Art. 7 Sect. VI of Basic Law for the Federal Republic of Germany) in Germany. Kids at kindergarten are not allowed to learn professional knowledge. It aims to avoid turning kids' brains into "Hard Disks" and leaves space for children to develop their imagination. The only task for kids before going to compulsory education is "grow up happily". "Play" is the natural instinct of children and it should not be disrupted. Three aspects need be addressed for a good education:

1. Common sense in society, e.g. violence prohibited.
2. Capability for "doing it by yourself", let kids get involved in arts & crafts production or other specific tasks according to their interests.
3. Develop emotional quotient, e.g. leadership.

In Germany, preschools are focused on "play". There is no subject-specific teaching or homework after school. Children develop autonomy from active play and sports. The teachers let the children lead the learning on their own behalf with necessary assistance and guidance. Children experiment and develop imagination by themselves. Germany is not the only country to adopt this rule; other European countries like Hungary, also prohibit children from learning writing, reading or calculation during the preschool stage. In fact, German schools do not put as much effort in addressing academic performance of students as Asian countries do when kids start the lower grade year in elementary school. They usually provide half day classes daily and there are two breaks for outdoor activities. Such a relaxing and pleasure class schedule surprisingly leads to high rankings in OEDC reports. Fifteen-year-old teenagers in Germany achieve excellent academic results that are well above international averages in reading, mathematics and science.

Perhaps Asian parents can change the education style for children and let kids learn interpersonal interaction and socialization from games, let kids try to reach anywhere they want to go, arrange celebrating parties at important moments of kids and take the kids out to play every day.

中文

　　亞洲國家家長普遍有不想讓孩子輸在起跑點的觀念存在，也大部分有「三歲定一生」的想法，相當重視學齡前教育或是較早就開始給予孩童傳統的正規學習，希望孩童能因相對較早學習及智力開發而能在日後有較高的成就。

　　在西方國家，有高成就的父母則被發現採取了與東方國家父母相反的教育方式，西方的學前教育很值得讓亞洲作為改善學前教育的參考。

　　以德國為例，在聯邦德國《基本法》（即憲法中第七條第六款）明確規定，禁止設立先修學校 (Vorschule)。幼兒園的孩子不允許學習專業知識，目的在避免將孩子大腦變成「硬盤」，要留給孩子更多想像空間，孩童在小學前的唯一任務就是「快樂成長」。他們認為孩子的天性是玩耍，所以不應該違背孩童的成長規律，若要進行教育的話，其重點應著重在以下三方面：

一、基本社會常識，如不允許暴力。
二、「動手能力」，讓孩子依自己的興趣參與手工製作或其他一些具體的事情。
三、培養孩子情緒智商，如領導力。

在德國，幼稚園的生活重心就是「玩」，並不進行分科教學，也沒有回家作業。他們在遊戲和運動中培養孩子的「自主性」，除了必要的協助和指引，每班老師們盡量讓孩子自己主導，自己去實驗和想像。不只德國有這樣的規定，其他歐洲國家也有類似情況，如匈牙利就嚴格禁止教授幼兒園期間的孩子學習寫作、閱讀、計算等。其實在上了小學後，德國的學校教育在低年級階段，也並不會像亞洲國家那般的強調學業表現，小學只上半天課，中間還有兩次戶外活動的休息時間。如此輕鬆愉快的課程安排，竟在經濟合作發展組織 (Organization for Economic Co-operation and Development) 的評鑑報告中，德國的 15 歲青少年在閱讀、數學、科學均有優於國際平均水準的表現。

也許亞洲的家長們可以改變方式，不教小朋友看書，讓小朋友從遊戲中學人際互動及社會化，讓小朋友嘗試自己去任何地方，辦派對慶祝孩子成長的重要時刻，每天都帶小朋友出去玩。

1　翻譯技巧

2　主題範例

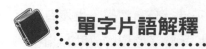 **單字片語解釋**

- perception *n.* 觀念、覺察力

  Kate changes our perception of reality.

  凱特改變了我們對現實的認知。

- abolish *v.* 廢除

  Many democracies have abolished capital punishment.

  很多民主國家已廢除死刑。

- compulsory *adj.* 強制性地、義務的

  It is compulsory for all motorcyclists to wear helmets.

  機車騎士強制性地應戴安全帽。

- instinct *n.* 本能、天性

  She should have trusted her own instinct.

  她應該相信她的直覺。

- quotient *n.* 商、商數

  Being rich doesn't actually increase your happiness quotient.

  有錢並無法提升幸福指數。

- autonomy　*n.*　自主權、自治、人身自由
  He sets a high value on autonomy.
  他對人身自由看得很重。

- socialization　*n.*　社會化、公有化
  Socialization of children was the primary function of the family.
  孩子的社會化是家庭功能的首務。

1 翻譯技巧

2 主題範例

🔍 相關句型翻譯要點

1. 原「以獲得諾貝爾獎人數佔總數的一半的德國為例，竟在聯邦德國《基本法》（即憲法中第七條第六款）明確規定，禁止設立先修學校 (Vorschule)...」譯作 "For example, pre-schools (Vorschule) were abolished in the constitutional rule (Art. 7 Sect. VI of Basic Law for the Federal Republic of Germany) in Germany." 當中的德國基本法，也就是德國的憲法，是德國的最高法，提及的法條是專有名詞，必須完全正確表示，不容錯誤。

2. 原「如此輕鬆愉快的課程安排，竟在經濟合作發展組織（Organization for Economic Co-operation and Development）的評鑑報告中，德國的 15 歲青少年在閱讀、數學、科學均有優於國際平均水準的表現。」譯成 "Such a relaxing and pleasure class schedule surprisingly leads to high rankings in OEDC reports. Fifteen-year-old teenagers in Germany achieve excellent academic results that are well above international averages in reading, mathematics and science." OECD 為 Organization for Economic Co-operation and Development 的縮寫，同篇文章中第一次出現的篇幅之後，就只需要直接寫縮寫的格式就可以了。

⭐ 前輩指點

　　翻譯是項經驗累積的工作，經驗雖是記在腦中，但其實人腦畢竟有極限，有些專有名詞久未接觸便會被大腦給擠出存放空間，哪天再度相遇時，又得再花一番時間搜索。而且現在網路資訊量爆多，搜索得在數以萬計的網頁中進行，才能找到滿意的答案。因此，除了工具書之外，筆者建議從事翻譯工作的譯者，自己還得準備一套屬於自己的分類筆記，而且最好是付諸電腦化的筆記。

　　筆記可粗略分為兩大類：一為針對資訊類或知識類較偏應用文體用字，二為偏文學性文體用字。知識類譯案偶有機會遇到相對冷門並不常涉獵的領域範圍內文章，光要查詢艱澀冷門字，可能就得耗費不少時間，趁著進行此類譯案的同時，整理編入自身筆記中，以後日久累積，此筆記也自然成為了自編工具書。

　　人文類或是較有文學性的翻譯，如小說，面對的字彙多半為敘述性用字，或是形容各種狀態或情境的用詞，也許在同一案件或是同本書中，會三不五時出現，若同樣的字，只用「有如、好像」來替代的話，易給人詞窮之感，若能以多組詞像是「就像、彷彿、宛如、恍如、恰似、好似、若、有若、好比、猶如、一如」等同義詞來替換，盡量將出現的間隔拉開，這樣譯出作品，自然要較為優質了。

主題 **6**

教育 6-2

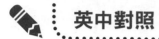 英中對照

Nordic countries usually get the higher rankings in the OEDC Better Life Index, and they get relatively positive reviews and higher satisfaction in the education system as well.

Demark was the first country which implemented education in Norden countries. It implemented compulsory 7-year education as far back as 1874, which is 100 year earlier than us. Even earlier than that, it set up the first folk high school in 1844. Danish adult education influences other Nordic countries.

Finland highlights its education in the higher education sector carrying forward to a good tradition within European Universities. The students of the University Student Associations in Finland enjoy the free and autonomous student life. The National Union of Finnish Students (SYL) is one of the richest, the most active, and most influential student associations in the world. It is not only capable of engaging in international exchange activities, but also is eligible to select representatives for attending conferences held overseas. Finland's junior high school education is well-known for its focus on most needed sectors, slow learners and students who need more care from the teachers. They utilize resources on the students who need them most. Finland emphasizes equal education instead of the elite education in most countries. This does its best to pull everyone up to the same status.

Sweden pays high attention to technology development in its education. It extended compulsory education to 9 years in 1950, which has been imitated by many other countries. The value and the meaning of setting up the Nobel Prize on science education are hard to define.

Norway's education performs well in leisure education. It is not only participated in by the whole nation but also well-organized in various aspects such as arts, music and literature. There are various options provided in society, and the educational principle is developed by the leisure education.

Iceland is a rich country with high income, and it has implemented 10-years compulsory education. It is one of the countries that eliminate illiteracy the earliest days. Iceland succeeds the great Viking literature traditions and talented writers appear continuously. The cultural life in the capital, Reykjavík is vigorous and riotous since the national theater was established in 1950. There are continuous national and international cultural events, and the international art festival is held every two years.

In the comparison of the above Nordic countries, they are in agreement on the implementation of education for all, advocating lifetime learning, maintaining anatomies and protecting the local culture. Looking at the current status of education in Taiwan, there is still a lot of space for improvement. Although Taiwan has put effort into the above perspectives, it must be doubly speeded up to improve so that the 100-year distance can be caught.

中文

常常在美好生活指數（OECD Better Life Index）排名趨前的北歐五國，教育制度也相對地得到正面評比與較高滿意度。

北歐五國中，丹麥是最早推行教育的國家，在 1874 年就已經有 7 年國民義務教育，早於我國百年以上。更早在 1844 年就有了第一所民眾高等學校，它的成人教育影響了其他北歐國家。

芬蘭的教育特色呈現在高等教育方面。大學生自治組織承繼了歐洲大學的優良傳統，享受自由、自治的生活，「芬蘭學生聯盟」是世界上最富有、最活躍，也最有影響力的學生自治組織。不僅有能力從事國際交流活動，並可派代表出國開會等等。芬蘭教育在國中階段以專注在最需要的地方著名，他們把資源運用在最需要老師關照的學生上。相較於很多國家把教育放在菁英身上，芬蘭強調的是平等教育，儘量把每個人都拉到同樣水平。

1

翻譯技巧

2

主題範例

　　瑞典的教育對「科技發展」最為重視，它在 1950 年時就將國民教育延伸為九年，各國也競相學習的改成九年。而其設立的諾貝爾獎在科學教育的意義與價值，更是難以估計。

　　挪威的教育則在「休閒生活教育」方面表現最好，不僅由全民參與，更在體育、美術、音樂、文學方面都有很好的安排，提供多樣選擇，由「休閒孕育文化」，來發展教育主軸。

　　冰島是高所得富國，實行十年制義務教育，是世上最早消除文盲的國家之一，繼承了古老維京文學傳統，文藝作家輩出。自 1950 年國家劇院落成後，首都雷克雅維克的「文化生活」多彩繽紛，國內、國際文化活動不斷，每兩年舉行國際藝術節。

　　相對比較起來，以上北歐五國在教育方面共同點為實施全民教育、倡導終身學習、維護自由氣氛及落實本土文化。反觀台灣現狀，的確是明顯的仍有很大的進步空間，雖說教育界已在上述各方面皆有著墨，但近百年的差距加上近年時勢變化快速劇烈，我們恐怕得以倍速努力改進，才能迎頭趕上。

1

翻譯技巧

2

主題範例

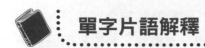

單字片語解釋

- Nordic   *adj.*   北歐人的
  Nordic companies are strong in technology and research and development.
  北歐企業在科技、研究、發展上很強。

- engage   *v.*   從事、使忙於
  He is engaged in doing the Spanish exercises.
  他正忙著他的西班牙語練習。

- elite   *n.*   精英份子
  Mark is supposed to be the elite of this school.
  馬克本應該是這學校的菁英分子。

- imitate   *v.*   仿效、學習
  The little girl imitates her mother's way of singing.
  這小女孩學她媽媽唱歌的方式。

- illiteracy　　*n.*　　文盲、失學
  It is our responsibility to help illiteracy.
  幫助文盲是我們的責任。

- perspective　　*n.*　　觀點、看法、洞察力
  His perspective was broader.
  他的眼界較寬。

1
翻譯技巧

2
主題範例

相關句型翻譯要點

1. 原「不僅有能力從事國際交流活動，並可派代表出國開會等等。」譯成 "It is not only capable of engaging in international exchange activities, but also is eligible to select representatives for attending conferences held overseas.", 此處除了使用 not only...but also... 來表達「不僅…並且…」的意涵，兩個在此段落的 it，是代名詞，代表的就是芬蘭的大學生自治組織。

2. 原「雖說教育界已在上述各方面皆有著墨，但近百年的差距加上近年時勢變化快速劇烈，我們恐怕得以倍速努力改進，才能迎頭趕上。」中的「雖然…但…」之意在此使用 although 來表達，譯作 "Although Taiwan has put effort into the above perspectives, it must be doubly speeded up to improve so that the 100-year distance can be caught."。

★ 前輩指點

　　其實有為數不少的翻譯從業人員，並非語文學系或是翻譯系所出身，不見得有很強的翻譯專業知識做堅實基礎來發展職涯，因此有些有意朝此方向發展的人，常有是否該進行翻譯相關學位進修的疑問，已有大學學位的人思考唸翻譯研究所的必要性，思忖著藉由更專精深入的研究所學習，讓自己的翻譯專業技能更上一層樓，更能得心應手地並更具說服力的接案。

　　其實資深人士建議可先思考一下以下幾個問題後再做打算：

　　現實面：剛出道的譯者收入不豐，稿費報酬欠個一兩個月很正常，而稿費水平近十幾年沒有上漲，新人要出頭得熬過一段很長的低薪陣痛期。翻譯研究所至少也得花上兩年時間，這兩年的生活費用會不會有問題，得先考慮清楚。

　　翻譯所是個講究實戰的研究所。除了中文底子，還要大量的時間投入練習。每天固定做練習或「一萬個小時的練習」這種定律幾乎是金科玉律。你可以保證以後的兩年每天都有時間練習翻譯嗎？若是真喜歡英文到無可自拔、享受翻譯，翻譯所歡迎你！

主題 **6**

教育 6-3

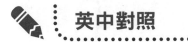

英中對照

The pusher of Taiwan's economy growth in the old days, technical and vocational education, has provided qualified personnel from agricultural and business schools to industry since the 50s when the agriculture and commodity industries started to develop. Some community colleges, five- year junior colleges, were set up between the 60s and 70s to train people for industrial development and economic development at the time as implementing the ten major construction projects. There are even more unsung heroes in the technical industry who made Taiwan become a State of Science and Technology cultivated by the vocational schools when the technical and petrochemical industry rose in the 80s and 90s. After entering the 21st century, the semi-conductor industry and panel industry-two trillion binary plan and the e-commerce applications led by the Internet boom making technology university students pushers for industrial development.

There is; however, maladjustment in these vacational schools that promoted technology colleges and universities' Four-year Completion Programs. The university act is not tailor-made for technical and vocational schools, and this leads to less cultivation of professional skills for teachers and students. They tend to focus on academic performance.

Another problem is that industry hires university graduates with the view of hiring community college students, but they cannot provide higher rewards and further plans for them. The third problem is that because industry develops more rapidly, it loosens the close relationship with the schools, which leads to talent shortage and talent mismatch in practice.

To solve these problems, the Ministry of Education started implementing the Reengineering Program for Technical and Vocational Education in 2010. It reinforces the practical and pragmatic characteristics of technical and vocational education, and it executed the second round of programs in 2013. There will be 20.2 billion dollars invested in 4 years and it focuses on adjusting the system, revitalizing the course and facilitating employment. It is expected to build up a better and more practical technology and vocational education by the further collaboration between industry and schools and the implementation of internship.

Nowadays the position for Taiwan's Technology and Vocational schools and Universities is unclear. It indeed is unnecessary for all schools to seek academic performance and recognition with the stature. Technology and vocational education should strengthen the linkage between the campus and the workplace by hiring more professional teachers from all walks of life through a multiple certification system. At the same time, the collaboration between industry and schools needs to be reinforced so that the school education and workplace practice can be smoothly linked up. The courses and certifications should be flexible and should break the fixed model of taking courses in schools. It advocates the technology and vocation education network combined with non-profit organizations, the workplace, training, and schools. Students not only take the course taught in the schools, but also address the capability for practical work. For example, some people who learn skills in the workplace can get the course credits through certain certifications.

The challenge for education is exactly the challenge for the whole nation, and it is not a single issue that the educational bureaucracy can deal with alone. For example, the repositioning of technology and vocational education is in a close relationship with the labor structure. There has to be cooperation with the Labor Department to work out the solution through inter-ministerial powers.

中文

　　昔日台灣經濟成長推手的技職教育，在 50 年代農業及民生工業興起時，有農校及商業學校培養人才供業界所用。在 60、70 年代推動十大建設之際，也有一些五專及工科學校，培養大批人才投入工業發展及經濟建設。80、90 年代科技產業及石化業興起之時，技專校院更是培養出為數不少的科技產業幕後英雄，讓台灣邁向科技大國。進入 21 世紀，半導體及面板業兩兆雙星計畫，及網路崛起帶動的電子商務及應用，更奠定了科大學生成為產業研發推手的形勢。

　　然而這些職校推升成技專校院地位後，卻有一些適應不良現象。其一是專科升格成四技科大，因大學法並沒有特別量身為技職打造，導致技職師資及學生在專業技能的培育偏少，轉而走向學術化。

　　其次是產業仍用過去聘用專科生的思維在聘用科大生，未能給予更高報酬及長遠的規畫。其三則是產業發展速度加快，與學校間的緊密合作關係漸趨疏離，趕不上業界步伐，導致學用產生落差。

　　為此教育部從 2010 年開始執行技職教育再造工程，強化技職教育務實致用、技能深耕的特性。2013 年更再執行第二期技職再造工程，在 4 年內投入 202 億經費，從調整制度、課程活化及促進就業等方面進行，進一步推動產學合作、落實學生實習，以期打造更優質、更務實的技職教育。

　　現在台灣的技職學校和大學，彼此定位並不是很清楚，其實不需要所有學校都去追求學術表現，成為有名大學，迷思應該要被打破。而技職教育強化校園和職場的連結，應由任用更多的技術教師，透過多元認證方式，廣泛地向各行各業徵求職業達人或師傅人才來達成。同時也要強化產學合作，讓

1
翻譯技巧

2
主題範例

學校教育和職場實務可以順利地銜接。職業教育授課課程與證書要能夠彈性化，打破只能在學校受教育的模式，倡導結合非營利組織、職場、職訓與學校的網絡式技職教育。學生修課不只限制於學校，更著重在實務能力。如在職場上學到技能的人，透過某種認證也能取得學分。

　　教育界的挑戰，其實是整個國家的挑戰，不是教育單位關起門來就能處理的事情，例如：技職體系的重新盤點和定位，跟勞動市場結構關係密切，必須跟勞動部門合作，更需用跨部會力量來共同解決問題。

單字片語解釋

- unsung　*adj.*　未被讚美的 , 未經承認的

  They are the unsung heroes of the Taiwan's economic miracle.

  他們是台灣經濟奇蹟的無名英雄。

- cultivate　*v.*　栽培、培養、教養

  Everyone should cultivate good manners from childhood.

  每個人都應該從小培養好禮貌。

- maladjustment　*n.*　失調、不適應

  It also provides guidance on maladjustment problems and parental education.

  它也針對失調問題及親職教育提供指導。

- tailor-made　*adj.*　量身打造的、訂製的

  This house is tailor-made for her.

  這棟房子是為她量身打造的。

- pragmatic　*adj.*　實際的、實用主義的

  They're pragmatic about cost-reduction.

  他們在降低成本方面很務實。

🔍 相關句型翻譯要點

1. 「進入 21 世紀，半導體及面板業兩兆雙星計畫，及網路崛起帶動的電子商務及應用，更奠定了科大學生成為產業研發推手的形勢。」翻作 "After entering the 21st century, the semi-conductor industry and panel industry - two trillion binary plan and the e-commerce applications led by the Internet boom making technology university students pushers for industrial development." 我們使用逗號來區分句子結構中的不同元素或句子，此處兩大不同元素即為半導體及面板業還有電子商務。

2. 「其三則是產業發展速度加快，與學校間的緊密合作關係漸趨疏離，趕不上業界步伐，導致學用產生落差。」譯為 "The third problem is that because industry develops more rapidly, it loosens the close relationship with the schools, which leads to talent shortage and talent mismatch in practice." ，which 在此代表前述子句中因產業發展速度加快而來的合作漸趨疏離現象。

3. 原「學生修課不只限制於學校，更著重在實務能力。如在職場上學到技能的人，透過某種認證也能取得學分。」譯為 "Students not only take the course taught in the schools, but also address the capability for practical work." ，not only...but also... 的使用，強調了「不只…更…」的意涵。

★ 前輩指點

　　筆者曾聽過有些在業界最前端打仗的翻譯公司坦言,在公司體制下有時是比在學校內還更容易訓練學生的,實戰場合是面對客戶時最立即的反應,通常也只有在真實戰場上,士兵才會感謝那隻送上彈藥補給的手,公司制度下有業績壓力,但也有相對得到報酬後的榮譽感激勵著培養中的譯手繼續奮戰下去。

　　以前台灣曾有相關翻譯系所學校曾成立翻譯公司,系上教授負責接案、連絡、協調、校稿,義務無償地做這些事情,結果反而造成學生畢業的錯誤認知:「沒有三元的案子不接。」,但殊不知若沒有老師幫學生批改校對送到客戶手上,那些學生連三毛都不值,另外隨之衍生出的「利用學校招牌接案就要上繳」心態,後來也造成了這種學生練兵系統無疾而終,而現在初入譯界的新手,常會有是否該加入翻譯社或翻譯公司的疑慮,深怕遇上血汗翻譯社或翻譯公司,成為被剝削的高級藍領,拿著偏低稿酬。不過,平心而論,自己的價值該由自己定義,賴以為之的就是你可以提供的服務—專業的翻譯能力。天下是絕對沒有白吃的午餐的。

主題 **6**

教育 6-4

英中對照

In the learning process for children, family education plays an important role in addition to formal school education. Enhancing the growth in a family environment outside of school cannot be ignored.

Researchers, anthropologists and children education experts at Harvard University have conducted a 20-year tracking survey of 456 teenagers in Boston. It was found that the unemployment ratio and crime ratio for the children who participate in household duties compared to those whom did not were 1:15 and 1:10. The children who took part in household duties earned an average income 20% higher than those who did not. The divorce rate and mental illness incidence for them was lower as well. Thus, it can be seen that people who had to participate in household duties and do tiring work from childhood get better achievement and happier lives. It is beneficial for kids throughout their lifetime if the parents create an environment to train them with chores from childhood. By virtue of enduring hardship and cherishing the fruits of labor and family, respect for other people will be developed.

There are following advantages for giving labor education to kids:
- Cultivate independence

Kids, after 1 year-old, tend to show the independency, and this "Do it myself" awareness can be developed healthily by taking one chores and household duties. Independence and creativity for kids is built up, and this works well so that they are able to do anything that they can without depending on other people in the future.

- Enhance combinatorial use of both hands and brain to develop intelligence

Physical labor has to be implemented by hands and brains. It makes the hands and brains develop coordinately by asking children to deal with basic and essential household duties in daily life. It is helpful for brain cells to be developed by stimulating the cells through the physical exercise.

- Improve health and constitution

Work can improve the development of muscles under a good nutrimental condition. The effect of work on developing a perfect physique is the same as sports.

- Build up virtue and a good personality

Early-chores education could train the children to cherish the fruits of labor. It makes children understand the real meaning of work building up the world, and this facilitates the development of great virtues and morals.

Here is one task list on household duties for American kids for information:

9-24 months - ask kids to throw dirty diapers into the rubbish cans.

2-3 years - throw rubbish into the cans under parent's supervision, help to fetch items for someone, use the toilet, brush teeth, water flowers and tidy up toys before sleeping.

3-4 year - use the toilet better, wash hands, brush teeth thoroughly, water flowers carefully, tidy up their own toys, go to the gate to fetch the newspaper on the ground, lay bedding for mother, put dishes into the kitchen sink after dinning, put dirty clothes into the basket.

4-5 years - fetch the letters in the postbox independently, lay the bedding by themselves, set the table, put the dirty dishes back in the kitchen, fold clean clothes then put them back in the closet (teach kids to fold the clothes correctly), prepare what they want to wear for the next day

5-6 years - wipe the table, make the bed / change bed sheets, prepare a schoolbag and shoes for the next day at kindergarten, clean the room.

6-7 years - wash the dishes under parent's supervision; clean own bedroom.

7-12 years - simple cooking, help to wash cars, vacuum and clean the floor, clean the restroom and toilet, sweep up leaves; use the washing machine and dryer, pull the rubbish can to the door.

13 years and above - change a light bulb, change the bag in the vacuum cleaner, wipe glasses (inside and outside), clean the fridge, clean the stove and oven, cook, make a shopping list, wash clothes (including wash, dry, fold and store the clothes), lawn care.

中文

　　孩子成長學習過程中，除了學校教育扮演重要角色外，家庭教育的配合相輔相成也是重要的環節，如何在學校教育外於家庭環境中幫助成長，不能不忽視。

　　哈佛大學曾有一些社會學家、行為學家和兒童教育專家，對波士頓地區456 名少年兒童進行了長達 20 年的跟蹤調查，發現愛做家務的孩子與不愛做家務的孩子相比較，長大後失業率比為 1：15，犯罪率比為 1：10，愛做家務的孩子平均收入高出 20% 左右，離異率、心理疾病患病率也較低。可見得從小做家務、熱愛勞動的人比從小不愛勞動的人較有工作成就，生活較美滿。父母若從孩提起為孩子創造一種環境和條件，對孩子進行早期勞動訓練，讓孩子做力所能及的事情，培養他們吃苦耐勞、珍惜勞動成果、珍重家庭親情、尊重他人等品質將可使其終身受益。

勞動教育對孩子有以下好處：

- 培養孩子的獨立性
　　一歲以後的孩子，會開始表現獨立意向，這種「我自己來」的獨立意識若能藉由勞動鍛鍊，學做家務來健康培養，可對孩子的獨立性與創造性起巨大作用，以後他就能「自己能做的事自己做，不依賴別人幫助」。

- 促進手腦並用，促進智力發育
體力勞動，是通過手腳活動來實現，對孩子要求最基本的生活自理和一些力所能及的家務等，可使其雙手和大腦協調發展。讓腦細胞得到更多刺激，加快腦細胞發育成長，將更有利於開發腦細胞。

- 促進身體健康、增強體質

在營養良好的情況下，勞動能促進肌肉的發育。勞動在培養完美體魄上所起的作用，同運動一樣重要。

- 促進良好個性品質的形成

對孩子進行早期勞動教育能培養孩子珍惜勞動成果，體會勞動創造世界的真實含義，從而促進良好個性、道德品質的發展。

至於家事活動的參與，倒是有份美國孩子家務清單，可供參考：

9-24 個月：可讓寶寶自己把髒的尿布扔到垃圾箱裡。

2-3 歲：在家長指示下把垃圾扔進垃圾箱，幫忙拿取東西，使用馬桶，刷牙，澆花，睡前整理自己的玩具。

3-4 歲：更好地使用馬桶，洗手，更仔細地刷牙，認真地澆花，收拾自己的玩具，大門口取回地上報紙，睡前幫媽媽鋪床，飯後自己把盤碗放到廚房水池裡，把自己的髒衣服放到裝髒衣服的籃子裡。

4-5 歲：獨自拿信箱裡的信，自己鋪床，擺餐具，把髒碗盤放回廚房，摺好衣服收回衣櫃裡（教孩子正確地摺衣服），自己準備隔天想穿的衣服。

5-6 歲：幫忙擦桌子，鋪床／換床單，自己準備第二天去幼兒園要用的書包和要穿的鞋，收拾房間。

6-7 歲：能在父母的幫助下洗碗盤，能獨立打掃自己的房間。

7-12 歲：能做簡單的飯，幫忙洗車，吸地擦地，清理廁所，掃樹葉，會用洗衣機和烘乾機，把垃圾箱搬到門口街上（有垃圾車來收）。

13 歲以上：能換燈泡，換吸塵器裡的垃圾袋，擦玻璃（裡外兩面），清理冰箱，清理爐台和烤箱，做飯，列待買清單，洗衣服（包括洗衣、烘乾衣物、疊衣以及放回衣櫃），修理草坪。

單字片語解釋

- household　*n.*　家庭的、家常的
  Parents should put education on the priority list of household affairs.
  父母必須視教育為重要的家務事。

- virtue　*n.*　美德、品行、能力
  He finally has the reward of virtue.
  他最後終獲善報。

- cultivate　*v.*　培養、栽培、養成
  We should cultivate the good habits of diligence.
  我們應該培養勤奮好習慣。

- combinatorial　*adj.*　組合的
  They are discussing a solution of combinatorial project.
  他們在討論這件組合計畫的解決方案。

- constitution　*n.*　體質、體格、結構
  Disease and hunger had weakened her constitution.
  疾病與飢餓已經削弱她的體質。

- physique　*n.*　體質、體魄
  Doing exercise helps us to strengthen the physique.
  運動幫助我們強化體魄。

相關句型翻譯要點

1. 原「哈佛大學曾有一些社會學家、行為學家和兒童教育專家，對波士頓地區 456 名少年兒童進行了長達 20 年的跟蹤調查，發現愛做家務的孩子與不愛做家務的孩子相比較，長大後失業率比為 1：15，犯罪率比為 1：10。」譯作 "Researchers, anthropologists and children education experts at Harvard University have conducted a 20-year tracking survey of 456 teenagers in Boston. It was found that the unemployment ratio and crime ratio for the children who participate in household duties compared to whom did not were 1:15 and 1:10." 此處涉及到數字的失業率與犯罪率比部分，我們同原文一樣，直接使用符號與阿拉伯數字表示，而不將 1:10 以 one to ten 英文字表達，因為通常以英文字表達的情況是建議用在 10（不包括 10）以下的數字。

2. 原中文沒有英語語法的時態與被動語態，我們在中翻英時必須看完整個句子後、段落，了解意思後再選擇適用的文法與時態譯出。

⭐ 前輩指點

　　翻譯產業中，價格不是很透明，許多翻譯社或翻譯公司並沒有公開訂價，而個人譯者也常沒有固定報價，讓很多客戶或是初入行新手對所謂的「翻譯行情價」或「適當合理的翻譯價格」完全沒有概念。客戶擔心價格過高，而低薪委託；譯者也可能因為擔心客戶砍價，反而事先哄抬價格，雙方討論報價時就好比是場拉鋸戰。

　　其實在此，倒是建議譯者能以公開透明的翻譯價格，讓客戶取得充分及對等資訊，幫助翻譯產業建立公定價格，更保障譯者能得到合理的報酬。一般筆譯服務的計價，是以「每字…元」計算（如：每字 2.5 元），接著再依字數計算總價。通常是以「原文字數」來計價，以避免爭議。若原文字數無法計算，（如：原文檔案為圖片檔），再考慮以「譯稿字數」另外譯價。目前若是翻譯經驗在三年以下的初級譯者，接一些不對外公開出版的案件行情價約介於 0.6~2 元／字間，而有三至 8 年經驗，曾有公開出版物的專業譯者，則有 2~3 元／字的行情，另外，有一些特殊要求或情況，如急件或超時等，也可視實際狀況調整。

主題 **6**

教育 6-5

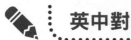

英中對照

Recently Taiwan's education sectors have been constantly undergoing reforms. The outcome of recent educational reform is that the Legislative Yuan third reading passed the Three-Type Acts of Experimental Education. In fact, there were developments in experimental education before the act received approval, such as forest schools, autonomic learning, Montessori education, and Waldorf education. They set up experimental school or educational organizations based on different regulations.

It is hard to provide this type of education to the majority of the population due to the higher cost counted at NTD20,000 monthly or the rush on transportation for picking up the kids though these kind of experimental organizations grow in a flourishing manner.

Fortunately, the Association of Parent Participating Education in Taiwan was officially established at the end of 2012. It created parent participating groups to initiate parent participating learning. It starts at the stage of young children then gradually extends to the elementary school and junior high school stages. It lowers the economic threshold with a unique model, and this allows more families with a general financial status to join the groups. Even blue-collar workers can afford it.

Every kid applies for entry individually; however, it is a group participation program, which shares the fees with the teachers. The classes are conducted locally around the whole province. There is no hardware or administrative staff. Parents from specific professions can provide lectures and it saves the administrative and teaching cost.

The target for the "large & little feet parents participating group" that the Association of Parent Participating Education promotes is mainly the parents or main caregivers who have young children aged between 0 and 5 years old. There are several groups formed in Hsinchu, Taipei, Tainan, Kaohsiung and Pingtung so far and they have spread to 12 cities in Taiwan. It is expected that there will be at least one group established in each city by 2016. Every group sets up a leader, who is in charge of all related staff and the allowance is donated by the families who participated. Each family pays NTD2,500 monthly at the preschool stage for 8 classes. As for the allowance of all administrative staff in the association, the leaders from all groups contribute 10% of the total income to it. For the elementary school and junior high school stages, each family pays an average of NTD8, 000 to 15,000 monthly for one child. The fee varies based on the different course themes.

It is required that every family takes an indoctrination and practice class before they join the group. The class includes discussion on concept clarification, experience sharing for parenting and parental interaction. There is no limit on the numbers of participants. Grandparents are also welcome.

At the young children stage, the main participating activities are book clubs and seminars. Parents need to firstly release their existing traditional educational concepts, which lead to bigger learning barrier. For children, all the parents should do is take them out for play.

Parents can join the book clubs for one year and observe their kids' capability based on the seven fields and ten indexes of Grade 1-9 Curriculums at the same time. By doing so, parents' anxiety in participating in this education can be eased. The parents who join the group have to participate in course planning or administrative work to develop the opportunity for running a school. They are not simply customers.

The unique operation model of the association for parents participating education makes the experimental education affordable. Whether it can accelerate as the experts predict really depends on how many parents are willing to change their concept and the way they raise their children.

中文

　　台灣的教育部門近年一直不斷有變革，近期一項最大的教育翻轉，就是立法院三讀通過的實驗教育三法。其實「實驗教育」在實驗教育三法通過前早有發展，除了最早起步的森林小學外，還有自主學習、蒙特梭利、華德福等教育模式，依據不同的法令，創立實驗學校或實驗教育機構。

　　這些實驗教育機構雖蓬勃發展，但對絕大多數家庭來說，每月動輒 2 萬元的學費或是奔波接送，仍是一大門檻，仍很難切實普及。

　　幸虧 2012 年底時，台灣親子共學教育促進會正式成立，倡議親子共學、開辦共學團體，從幼兒共學開始，逐步推展到國小、國中共學，其獨創的模式降低共學的經濟門檻，連藍領階級都付得起，讓更多經濟能力一般的家庭能一起加入。

1
翻譯技巧

2
主題範例

共學團體中每個孩子都是以申請個人自學的方式加入，但實質上是團體共學，分攤專業老師的費用；而且上課模式是全省移動，沒有學校硬體、行政人員，有特定專業、能做講師的父母也共同分攤掉不少教學、行政的費用。

親子共學教育促進會推動的「大腳小腳親子共學團」招收對象，主要是家中有 0 ～ 5 歲幼兒的父母或主要照顧者，目前已在新竹、台北、台南、高雄、屏東等地開團，足跡遍及全台 12 個縣市，預計 2016 年全國各縣市至少會有 1 個共學團。每一個親子共學團設有領隊，統籌一切相關事務，其津貼是由參與共學的家庭捐款，學前階段每戶每月繳 2500 元、每個月共學 8 次，而親子共學教育促進會的所有行政人員，再由共學團領隊捐出所得的 10% 來支應。至於國小、國中共學部分，因為每月主題課程的費用不同，每月每戶一個小孩平均約需花費 8000 ～ 1 萬 5000 元。

每個家庭加入共學團之前，必須先參加「教養實踐班」課程，包含理念澄清討論、育兒經驗分享、親子互動體驗等內容，每戶不限上課名額，除了爸媽外，也歡迎阿公、阿嬤一起來。

　　幼兒階段的親子共學,主要帶領父母或幼兒照顧者進行讀書會、舉辦課程講座等,因為爸媽本身帶有很多傳統既定的教育觀念,學習阻礙較大,所以需要先「釋放」觀念,而小孩只要帶出去玩就好了。

　　而參加小學共學之前,父母方面須進行長達一年的讀書會,同時還要根據九年一貫課程的 7 大領域、10 大指標,觀察自家小孩所具備的能力狀況。這是為了解除父母對於參加共學的焦慮。參加親子共學的父母,必須參與、分擔課程的規劃設計或行政工作,讓父母也有機會辦學校,而不是來消費的。

　　親子共學教育促進會獨特的運作模式,讓實驗教育費用平價化,但是否能如專家預料加速成長,還要看願意改變觀念和作法的父母有多少了。

單字片語解釋

- caregiver　*n.*　照顧者、提供照料的人
  Housewives are usually the primary caregivers of the elder in the family.
  家庭主婦常是家中老人家的主要照顧者。

- allowance　*n.*　零用錢、津貼、補助
  My dad used to give us allowance every month.
  我爸爸過去每個月都會給我們零用錢。

- indoctrination　*n.*　教養
  The media attempt to convey green indoctrination to the public.
  媒體試圖傳播環保意識給大眾。

- barrier　*n.*　障礙、阻隔
  She soon overcame the language barrier.
  她很快地克服語言障礙

- accelerate　*v.*　加速、促進
  The driver accelerated the bus running through the red light.
  公車司機加速，闖了紅燈。

相關句型翻譯要點

1. 原「這些實驗教育機構雖蓬勃發展，但對絕大多數家庭來說，每月動輒 2 萬元的學費或是奔波接送，仍是一大門檻，仍很難切實普及。」譯出成 "It is hard to provide this type of education to the majority of the population due to the higher cost counted at NTD20,000 monthly or the rush on transportation for picking up the kids though these kind of experimental organizations grow in a flourishing manner." 此處的 It 為虛主詞，代表的即是實驗教育機構。

2. 「每一個親子共學團設有領隊，統籌一切相關事務，其津貼是由參與共學的家庭捐款…2500 元」翻作 "Every group sets up a leader, who is in charge of all related staff and the allowance is donated by the families who participated." 此處 who 即為前述的負責人，也就是領隊人物。

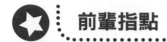

前輩指點

　　筆者本身並非翻譯本科系學生畢業，當初接觸翻譯工作時，也沒有特別因緣際會認識前輩領著，一切好像就是一股「翻就對了」的態勢，經由不斷的翻譯來練出實力，相對地也不是很清楚有哪些接案管道，好讓自己可在累積實力的同時，也或多或少有少許收入。

　　而現在相對於之前的情況，在台灣似乎接案來源頗多元化，不至於有喝西北風之虞。

　　以下幾個案件來源管道，可以試試，多多撒網，總能抓到個一兩尾魚！

　　PTT BBS 站有個「翻譯版」，價碼與案件時間相對合理，可自己直接與案主聯繫溝通，合作默契佳的話，一試成主顧，日後案主或許還會回鍋。但因為 PTT 高手頗多，所以也算競爭激烈。

　　其二為就業網站 104 / 518 等本地的外包網，這種外包平台主要缺點是要先付一筆平台費用，投資報酬率得再多多評估，不過，看自己如何運用了，我相信這種平台上的機制是有些方法可運用來提高回復率與接案率的。

　　第三個案件來源則為翻譯社，但是通常翻譯社抽成相對高很多，可對於新手而言，增加練筆機會大過於實質報酬，一旦合作穩定上軌後，案源將會增多，不怕斷炊。

　　另外，就是一般公司／協會的翻譯了，這類型翻譯工作的好處是薪水穩定，並有固定的勞健保及一般上班族的福利。

　　另外，取得案件機率相對低的管道還有朋友介紹、編輯找人、前輩引薦等，最後還可試試國外的平台及／翻譯社／翻譯社團，通常國外的最低價碼會約莫等同於國內的合理價碼，但是平台費用與國內的平台相比，也著實是相對高的。

主題 **7**
動畫 7-1

 英中對照

Although animation movies do not represent the majority of movie genres, their status should not be underestimated from the view of the development trend of the modern movie industry. Though the eastern animation industry is not as long established and complete as the western one, it has built up its base to a certain level. Studio Ghibli, led by animation master, Miyazaki Hayao and Takahata Isao is the most representative studio in Japan.

Studio Ghibli was established in June, 1985. Its initial intention was provide a workplace for Miyazaki Hayao and his partner, Takahata Isao to solve the distribution problems of "Nausicaä of the Valley of the Wind" for the production team. Its works are exquisite, lively and filled with imagination. It has won the prestigious reputation around the world with its continuously high-quality works though it went through several organizational restructurings.

Among the masterpieces that Studio Ghibli has released is "Laputa: Castle in the Sky". It was derived from British writer Jonathan Swift's novel "Gulliver's Travels", where Laputa is a castle on a flying island. Many settings are similar to ancient civilizations, like the huge robots, and it makes the experience fascinating and unforgettable. There is no doubt it has become no. 1 on the list of Miyazaki Hayao's works on the Internet.

"My Neighbor Totoro" is another famous work that describes the original natural beauty of Japan before its advanced economic development. It is full of the incredible world that can only be seen by children and those with a rich imagination. It is very popular because of the rousing nostalgia it brings to the audiences. "My Neighbor Totora" is Miyazaki Hayao's representative work; therefore, Studio Ghibli takes the head portrait of Totoro as its theme in its logo and mascot.

"Spirited Away" is another of Miyazaki Hayao's works which achieved the highest recognition. It also called "Miyazaki Hayao version of Alice's Adventures in Wonderland". In the movie he wishes to attach great importance to several friends' daughters and for them to affirm their own capability. This animation has won many prizes that include the Best Film at Japan Academy Prize in 2001 and Berlin Film Festival Golden Bear in 2002 (first animation winner in history). It won the 75th Academy Award for Best Animated Feature Film and the 68th New York Film Critics Circle Award for Best Animated Film in 2002. It is also the best seller in the history of Japanese movies. It definitely is a hot work of Miyazaki Hayao.

The master, Miyazaki Hayao specifically emphasizes the relationship between human beings and the natural environment. His works are not only pure entertaining animations but also meaningful education films. Besides, the delicate stories, their meanings are revealed by the fine hand-painted animation without depending on technology too much. All this creates the unique enduring attraction of Miyazaki Hayao's works, and helps them maintain popularity as lasting gems.

中文

　　動畫電影雖不是占最大宗的電影類型，但從近代電影業發展趨向來看，地位亦不容小覷。東方的動畫產業發展雖不若西方這般悠久且完整，但亦已經建構了一定基礎。最具代表性的應該就算是在日本，以動畫大師宮崎駿及高畑勳為主力的吉卜力工作室了。

　　吉卜力工作室成立於 1985 年 6 月，原成立的意旨乃是要提供一個讓宮崎駿及其動畫搭檔前輩高畑勳專用的動畫製作場所，以解決原《風之谷》動畫製作團隊解散的問題。而後雖歷經數次組織變動，但吉卜力仍然持續推出高品質作品，細膩富有生氣外，還充滿了想像力，在全世界獲得極高的評價。

　　吉卜力推出的部部佳作中，《天空之城》引用英國作家喬納森・斯威夫特 1726 年的小說《格列佛遊記》中的飛島國空中城堡拉普達 (Laputa) 為舞台，許多設定也類似古文明，如巨大的機器人等等，使人非常嚮往難忘，成為網路人氣第一的宮崎駿作品實不為過。

　　而另一部名作《龍貓》描繪的是日本在經濟高度發展前存在的美麗自然，充滿只有孩子才能看見的不可思議世界和豐富想像，因喚起了觀眾的鄉愁而廣受歡迎，為宮崎駿的成名代表作，吉卜力工作室的商標與吉祥物，因此採用龍貓的造型頭像作主視覺。

1
翻譯技巧

2
主題範例

另一部可說是最高成就的宮崎駿作品為《神隱少女》，此片又稱為「宮崎駿版的愛麗絲夢遊仙境」。他希望能藉此片鼓動幾名朋友的女兒去重視並肯定自己的能力，此部動畫獲得許多獎項，2001 年獲得日本電影金像獎最佳影片獎，2002 年獲得柏林影展金熊獎（史上首部獲得該獎項的動畫片），更在2002 年贏得第 75 屆奧斯卡金像獎最佳動畫長片獎，及 68 屆紐約影評人協會的最佳動畫獎，目前也是日本影史上票房最高的電影，可說是宮崎駿的熱門代表作。

宮崎駿大師的作品，特別著重在處理人類與大自然間互動的關係，使得他的作品不只是單純娛樂動畫片，更是富含意義的教育片。此外，精緻的劇情設定與意涵，經由細膩手繪動畫表現，不依賴過多的科技技術，在在塑造了宮崎駿動畫的獨特雋永吸引力，讓這些老動畫片的人氣能歷久彌新。

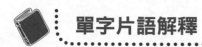

單字片語解釋

- animation　*n.*　動畫、生氣、活潑
  This film was the first Australian animation sold to an American network.
  這是第一部賣給美國電視網的澳洲動畫。

- exquisite　*adj.*　精緻的、細膩的
  She painted an exquisite painting.
  她畫了一幅精緻的油畫。

- prestigious　*adj.*　受尊敬的、有聲望的
  Peter graduated from a prestigious university.
  彼得畢業於一所名校。

- fascinating　*adj.*　著迷的、被深深吸引的
  The city is fascinating.
  這座城市很迷人。

- capability　*n.*　能力
  The kid has capability of being an outstanding ballet dancer.
  那孩子擁有成為傑出芭蕾舞者的能力。

🔍 相關句型翻譯要點

1. 原「動畫電影雖不是占最大宗的電影類型，但從近代電影業發展趨向來看，地位亦不容小覷。東方的動畫產業發展雖不若西方這般悠久且完整，但亦已經建構了一定基礎。」中有兩結構相似，並且也含有雖然…但…含意的句子，所以我們翻出 Although animation movie does not represent the most majority of movie genres, its status should not be underestimated from the view of development trend for modern movie industry. Though the eastern animation industry is not as long and completed as western one, it has built up certain levels of base to grow." 以 although(though) 為首的兩句子來傳達語意。

2. 「…他的作品不只是單純娛樂動畫片，更是富含意義的教育片…」譯成 "His works are not only pure entertaining animations but also meaningful education films...", 在此我們使用 not only...but also... 來表示不只是…更是…的含意。

⭐ **前輩指點**

一般來講，大部分發案方在決定譯者前，都會進行試譯，從中選擇最能達到預定要求的譯者才發案，理應中選的譯者譯出的文不大需要大幅度的修改，但是不怕一萬，只怕萬一，也許有時有一些無法預想的狀況發生，而使得必須將譯稿重修，因此我們也該有些預防或是因應的方法來幫助自己仍能圓滿達成任務。

要事先預防；試譯稿或許符合要求，可是整本書是否都能維持一樣的水準，仍是未知。為了避免這種狀況，在案件一開始，最好能在翻譯合約上明訂改稿約定，例如，若譯稿不符合編輯預期的標準，至少一次無償改稿。針對錯誤的容許程度，一開始也要設立標準。

要虛心就教、努力溝通；翻譯沒有絕對的答案，也沒有完美無缺的譯稿，對於拉近編輯與譯者雙方對風格的期待，建議可以翻譯了前面一或兩個章節後，先傳給編輯預覽，若有批評指教或需要修改之處，可趁早溝通。

經過事先預防、虛心就教、努力溝通以及共同決定處理方式之後，如果編輯與譯者仍無法達成共識，或許，雙方就只能接受結果了。

主題 **7**

動畫 7-2 ────

✏️ 英中對照

When speaking of animation movies, we cannot fail to mention Walt Disney in the USA, which is positioned as the leading role model in the industry. It was initially established as "Disney Brothers Cartoon Studio" by Walt Disney and Roy Disney on Oct. 16th , 1923. The famous animation character, Mickey Mouse, was the major image identity of the company in the early years.

The Walt Disney Company set up its base with animation. Its "Snow white and Seven Dwarfs" released in 1937, was the first color full-length animated film in the world. Then, as the leading player, it released various genres of motion pictures throughout the following several decades and it gradually expended into a multinational corporation. Among the works released by the corporation the most representative of Walt Disney Animation Studios are called "Walt Disney's CLASSICS", and they are also the signature works of Disney. "CLASSICS" include traditional hand-drawn animation and 3D computer animation. "Chicken Little" released in 2005 is the dividing line between them. The works before "Chicken Little" are hand-drawn animations; the work after it are mostly computer-animated even 3D featured. Most Disney animations are full-length comedy-drama films, and some of them are adapted for the parades at Disneyland, Disney On Ice and Disney On Stage. They have even released TV series and audio & video products sequels.

There are 55 films in this CLASSICS as of March, 2016. "Frozen", released in 2013, is the most successful animated motion picture in history. It not only won various prizes like the 71st Golden Globe Award for Best Animated Feature Film, the 41st Annie Award for Best Animated Feature, the 67th British Academy Film Awards for Best Animated Film, and the 86th Academy Award for Best Animated Feature Film and Best Original Song Let It Go. It also grabbed big success at the box office. Total worldwide sales reached USD1.27 billion, which is also the seventh Disney's film that earned over 1 billion. "Forzen" was the top movie worldwide in 2013 and it is listed as the 9th highest revenue film in movie history. The Walt Disney Company indeed accomplished a lot by this film.

中文

　　說到動畫電影，就不能不提位於業界領導地位的美國華特迪士尼公司，該公司最初稱為「迪士尼兄弟動畫工作室」，成立於 1923 年 10 月 16 日，由華特‧迪士尼和洛伊‧迪士尼所建立，早期知名的動畫形象—米奇老鼠就是華特迪士尼公司最主要的形象象徵。

　　華特迪士尼公司以動畫奠基，1937 年推出的「白雪公主」是世界第一部彩色長篇動畫電影，從此迪士尼成為動畫龍頭，數十年來幾乎年年推出不同類型的動畫電影，逐漸由原本的動畫工作室擴張為跨國公司，當中最具代表性的「華特迪士尼動畫片廠」（Walt Disney Animation Studios）推出的作品，就被稱為「迪士尼經典動畫」（Walt Disney's CLASSICS）。它同時也是迪士尼的招牌作品，包括了傳統手繪動畫和 3D 電腦動畫，以 2005 年的《四眼天雞》為分野，《四眼天雞》以前的作品都是傳統手繪動畫，之後的則多為電腦製圖動畫，並且大都也製作了 3D 版本。迪士尼動畫大部分為長篇劇情片，不少作品後來還改編為迪士尼樂園的遊行表演、冰上世界、音樂劇等，甚至有電視版影集或影音產品續集。

　　截至 2016 年 3 月份止，此經典系列共有 55 部之多，在經典系列中，2013 年出品的《冰雪奇緣》可說是目前為止，史上最成功的動畫電影，不僅獲得多項獎項如：第 71 屆金球獎最佳動畫片、第 41 屆安妮獎最佳動畫電影、第 67 屆英國電影學院獎最佳動畫電影，及第 86 屆奧斯卡金像獎最佳動畫長片和最佳原創歌曲《Let It Go》；更在票房上也獲佳績，全球各地共賣了 12.76 億美元，是有史以來最高票房的動畫片，迪士尼電影公司第七部超過 10 億美元的影片。是 2013 年度全球最高票房電影，並且在世界電影史上列居收入第 9 高的電影，成就非凡。

單字片語解釋

- decade　*n.*　十年
  He has attempted a complete control over his business for decades.
  過去十年他嘗試完全掌握自己的事業。

- signature　*n.*　署名、簽名、識別標誌
  Beef stew is one of chef MumMum Su's signature dishes.
  燉牛肉是主廚蘇嬤嬤的招牌菜。

- genre　*n.*　類型
  Animated movie is the most popular genre of movie for children.
  動畫電影是最受孩童歡迎的電影類型。

- featured　*adj.*　有⋯面貌特徵的、作為特色的
  The kid looked sharp-featured.
  小孩看起來五官分明。

- sequel　*n.*　續集、續篇、結局
  The audience expected the male supporting role can appear in the sequel of the movie.
  觀眾期待這個男配角會在電影續集中出現。

- accomplish　*v.*　使完美、完成
  She accomplished her goal and won the contest.
  她達成她的目標，並贏得比賽。

相關句型翻譯要點

1. 「說到動畫電影，就不能不提…美國華特迪士尼公司…」譯作 Speaking animation movie, we cannot fail to mention...Walt Disney in USA..."

2. 「當中最具代表性的『華特迪士尼動畫片廠』（Walt Disney Animation Studios）推出的作品，就被稱為『迪士尼經典動畫』」譯作 "Among of the corporation, the works released by the most representative Walt Disney Animation Studios are called "Walt Disney's CLASSICS..." 在此使用 among 此介詞乃是因為此情況適用於三個或三個以上的標的物，迪士尼一系列作品超過三個以上，故使用 among 來表示三個以上的當中。

3. 中文表示 12.76 億美元時，翻成英文則為 USD1.27 billion，以數字配合單位來表示美元，美元是辨識率高的貨幣，可以僅用符號表示，而遇到其他一些辨識率不高的貨幣時，就得譯出英文名稱了。像是俄羅斯的貨幣盧布就得譯出 ruble。

⭐ 前輩指點

　　從筆者幾年下來的經驗中，有不少與翻譯從業人士及相關出版社的交流，大家或多或少都會聊到不受歡迎的譯者是什麼樣子，歸納出以下幾種類型，給有志成為優秀譯者的人士參考，避免踩到地雷而讓專業翻譯職業生涯終止。

　　以下為合夥人最不希望在譯者身上看到的缺點，供有志於成為優秀譯者的朋友參考並引以為戒：

- 缺乏職業責任心
- 不誠實
- 不嚴謹、不求甚解、粗心大意 - 專業翻譯絕對不能有前述這三大致命傷。
- 不積極解決問題
- 不能保守客戶秘密。若接的案子涉及企業營運策略面，就應恪守職業道德，替顧客保守商業機密。
- 不能完成已承諾的工作
- 不守時

主題 7
動畫 7-3

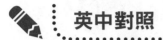
英中對照

1974 witnessed a change in the production process of animated films, with the long standing Academy Awards introducing a catergory for Animated Short Film. The rise of 3D animation films was observed during the decade. 3D computed animations represent almost all animation films nowadays.

Pixar Animation Studios, Blue Sky Studios and DreamWorks SKG are currently famous 3D animation studios. Pixar among the above has operated well and achieved diligent results. It is the most successful animation studio in the world.

Pixar's predecessor was part of the computer division of Lucasfilm that was established in 1979. Pixar Animation Studios was purchased in 1986 by Apple Inc. co-founder, Steve Jobs. It is located in Emeryville, California and it also produces 3D software like PRman. Pixar was then acquired by the Walt Disney Company in 2006 at a valuation of 7.4 billion US dollars. Jobs became the largest individuals shareholder at the time.

Pixar has released 15 full-length animated films as of 2013. Thirteen of the works gained positive reviews and commercial success. It has won twenty-seven Academy Awards, seven Golden Globe Awards, eleven Grammy Awards and many others as of 2014. It has earned 7 Academy Awards for Best Animated Feature since the award started in 2001 including *Finding Nemo, The Incredibles, Ratatouille, WALL-E, UP, Toy Story 3, Brave. Monsters, Inc.* and *Cars* are the only two films that were nominated for the award without winning it.

In addition, all fourteen works earned at least an "A" rating from Cinema Score, which showed high acceptance from audiences. Pixar's works have earned 8.5 billion US dollars as of December, 2013. Each film made an average of 607 million US dollars. They all are among the 50 highest-grossing animated films, and *Finding Nemo* and *Toy Story 3* remain in the 50 highest-grossing films all the time. *Toy Story 3* even took 1 billion US dollars worldwide.

中文

　　從 1974 年開始設立，有著長遠歷史的奧斯卡最佳動畫短片獎項，見證了動畫產業改變的過程，近十年來的最佳動畫短片及提名影片，更讓我們目睹了 3D 動畫片的興起，似乎 3D 電腦動畫取代了一切。

　　皮克斯動畫工作室、藍天工作室、夢工廠等是目前比較著名的 3D 動畫工作室，其中又以皮克斯表現最為亮眼，成就卓越，可說是全球最成功的動畫公司。

　　皮克斯動畫工作室的前身是盧卡斯影業於 1979 年成立的電腦動畫部，1986 年時被蘋果公司聯合創始人史提夫・賈伯斯收購，位於加州愛莫利維爾市。該公司也製作電腦 3D 軟體，如 PRMan。2006 年時皮克斯更被迪士尼以 74 億美元收購，成為華特迪士尼公司的一部分，賈伯斯亦因此成為迪士尼的最大個人股東。

截至 2013 年，皮克斯共發布了 15 部動畫長片，有 13 部都獲得好評與商業上的成功。皮克斯至 2014 年已獲得 27 次奧斯卡獎、7 次金球獎、11 次葛萊美獎以及其他獎項。自 2001 年奧斯卡最佳動畫片獎設立以來，皮克斯電影有七部獲獎，分別是《海底總動員》、《超人特攻隊》、《料理鼠王》、《瓦力》、《天外奇蹟》、《玩具總動員 3》及《勇敢傳說》；還有兩部《怪獸電力公司》與《汽車總動員》獲得提名。

此外，皮克斯的 14 部作品都獲得了 Cinema Score 至少「A」的評價，表示觀眾對其作品的接受度很高。截至 2013 年 12 月，該公司的所有作品在全世界累計獲得了 85 億美元的票房，平均每部電影獲得 6.07 億美元。皮克斯電影都曾進入電影票房收入前五十名，其中《海底總動員》與《玩具總動員 3》一直保持在前五十名，《玩具總動員 3》已在全球獲得了十億美元票房。

 單字片語解釋

- witness　*v.*　目睹、見證
  None could witness that she was present.
  沒有人能見證她在場。

- predecessor　*n.*　前任、前身
  Peter was more successful than his predecessor.
  彼得比起他的前任更有成就。

- acceptance　*n.*　接受、認可
  His music has not found general public acceptance.
  他的音樂尚未獲得大眾的廣泛認可。

🔍 相關句型翻譯要點

1. 「其中又以皮克斯表現最為亮眼，成就卓越，可說是全球最成功的動畫公司。」譯作 "Pixar among the above has operated well and achieved diligent results. It is the most successful animation studio in the world." 使用 among 而不是其他介系詞，如 between，是因為 among 「在⋯之中」適用在三者或三者以上的情況。

2. 「此外，皮克斯的 14 部作品都獲得了 Cinema Score 至少「A」的評價⋯」譯作 "In addition, all fourteen works earned at least an "A" rating from Cinema Score..." 我們使用 in addition 來表示「此外」，屬性為副詞，完整意思是「除了⋯以外，還有⋯」，不是只有當前現在這件事物而已，此句後方之後的事物都被包含在內，其他副詞如 on top of that 也同樣用法。

★ 前輩指點

　　翻譯其實算是件苦差事，累積經驗，不斷的翻翻翻是該下的基本功，熱情與持續力是造就專業的必要條件，跟學習外語一樣，我想應該有不少的人，藉由從事自己喜歡有興趣範圍內的事物來維持其專業領域內的持續經營力，不少熱愛西洋音樂的人，因為想懂歌詞意思、想學會那首最愛的西洋歌曲，而努力學英文。而相信有不少筆譯從業人員，一開始的入門，就是從漫畫或動畫來著手的。

　　漫畫或動畫，字數通常不太多，又配有圖像，通常很容易可讓譯者首先達到信、雅、達當中的「信」，不大容易有錯譯的情形發生，而漫畫或動畫題材，通常趣味性較足，避免枯燥乏味而漸漸失去興趣。而相當仰賴「日起有功」，每日或是規律性的產出及養成翻譯的習慣，對一位專職翻譯而言是相當重要的。初入翻譯領域的新手，初期訓練及經營自己的方式，倒是可以先從翻譯漫畫開始，漫畫的篇幅都不太長，每天或隔幾天規律的要求自己翻個幾幅漫畫，維持翻譯習慣，天天練功。國內翻譯界就有不少傑出譯者，一開始以漫畫的翻譯及經營部落格的方式來累積實力而漸漸闖出名號，成為譯界中一把交椅。

主題 **7**

動畫 **7-4**

英中對照

As for the animation industry, apart from mainstream animated films that we frequently talk about, there're other forms of animated films that exist in other non-movie forms. Many supporters and enthusiasts maintain their success and develop them in multiple models, especially in Japan, which has its own independent financing.

There are about 430 animated studios in Japan. GAINAX and Toei Animation Co., Ltd. are the ones with better popular recognition aside from the most famous Studio, Ghibli, which is related to Miyazaki Hayao animation. These studios have different focuses, for example TV Animation, Movie Animation, OVA (Original Video Animation) and Net animation according to the broadcast medium.

Most Japanese animations are adapted from comics, and originals are secondly. More and more animations are being adapted from video games and light novels in recent years. The material coverage is diverse. The first popular animation series "Astro Boy" was the work of cartoonist, Tezuka Osamu during the early development of Japanese animation. During the 1970s, the Japanese developed unique types of animation like robot animation. "Mazinger Z" and "Tetsujin 28-go" are famous works during this period. Many animations are produced in large numbers. Some of them are origins; some of them are adaptations. The master, Miyazaki Hayao made a great coup after the 70s. The animation series like "Neon Genesis Evangelion" and "Ghost in the Shell: Stand Alone Complex" not only attracted attention from Japanese audiences but also caught the eye of overseas audiences. "Dragon Ball", "Sailor Moon" and "Pokemon" merchandise are also popular in European and American regions.

The most unique characteristics of the Japanese animation industry that is different from other regions is the derivatives of subculture. Sometimes subculture becomes the mainstream movement although it is related to minor events. Cosplay is an example of the subculture which is related to animation.

Cosplay originated in the Comic Market, also called Comiket, Comike or CM. It has been one of the biggest Japanese dōjinshi fairs since the late 1970s. The participants dress up like popular characters of that time. Some say; however, that there is a rival to Japan coming from Science Fiction Convention in the USA where the participants play the roles in "Star Trek". The reality is nuclear. It is said that cosplay became more famous when the animation, Neon Genesis Evangelion gained favorable reviews during the mid-1990s and then became the focus of widespread attention. At the same time, commercial activities started development at cosplay events. Some clothing manufacturers started the commercialization of cosplay clothing that used to be made by individuals. Today, cosplay has gradually become one single main events instead of many affiliated events being held at the same time. It is no longer the collection of events that it used to be.

中文

說到動畫產業，除了我們常提及的主流動畫電影外，也有其他不少非電影形式的動畫產品存在發展著，並且也有為數不少的支持者及愛好者支撐著其存續，甚至多元發展，自成一經濟規模，特別是日本。

日本的動畫界約有 430 家動畫工作室，除了較著名的因宮崎駿相關動畫電影大出風頭的吉卜力工作室外，GAINAX 及東映動畫也算是較知名的，而這些工作室發展的主力皆有不同，依播放媒介來劃分的話，從電視動畫、劇場版動畫、OVI 原創動畫錄映帶到網路動畫，都有工作室在從事著。

日本動畫多數由漫畫改編，其次才是原創，但近年來也有越來越多動畫是由電玩和輕小說改編，取材相當多元。日本動畫發展初期時，第一套廣泛流行的連續劇《原子小金剛》即是漫畫家手塚治蟲的作品。1970 年代間，日本的動畫有別於西方發展出獨特類型，如機器人動畫，較出名的作品有《無敵鐵金剛》及《鐵人 28 號》，在此之後大量產出，有些是改編的，有些是原創的，大師宮崎駿就是在這之後大獲成功的，此時期的動畫連續劇如《新世紀福音戰士》、《攻殼機動隊》在日本大受歡迎外，也吸引了海外觀眾注意力。《七龍珠》、《美少女戰士》和《神奇寶貝》等發展的周邊商品在歐美地區也受到大大的歡迎。

日本動畫業另外最不同於其他地區動畫業的特點，即是次文化的衍生，雖說是次文化，但在日本有時反而有躍升為主流之勢。Cosplay 即為與動畫相關的次文化例子。

　　Cosplay 起源自 1970 年代後半的 Comic Market，又稱 Comiket、Comike 或 CM，是日本最大的同人展會活動，參加者打扮成當時流行的動畫角色模樣。雖然有人說其實這種活動是源起自美國舉辦的日本科幻大會，參加者打扮成《星艦迷航記》中的人物，但實際情況不明。而 Cosplay 更廣為人知據說是在 1990 年代中期左右，由於動畫《新世紀福音戰士》大受好評，而成了眾人注目焦點並隨之跟著普及。而同時，商業運作也開始在 Cosplay 活動上開展，一些成衣或是服飾製造商開始將此向來為私人製作的 Cosplay 用服飾商品化並販售。時至今日，本來都只是在相關活動時順便從事的 cosplay，也漸漸地有單獨活動，不再只是附屬活動。

 單字片語解釋

- enthusiast　*n.*　愛好者、熱衷者
  Paul is a skiing enthusiast.
  保羅是個滑雪運動愛好者。

- adapt　*v.*　改編、改寫
  This play is adapted from a novel.
  這齣劇改編自一本小說。

- derivatives　*n.*　衍生物
  Futures is one of the derivative financial products.
  期貨是一種衍生性金融商品。

相關句型翻譯要點

1. 「說到動畫產業…」中，我們使用 As for 來譯出「說到」，同時也可視作為「至於，就…方面來說」是個介系詞，用法上常放在句首，亦有轉換語氣的作用。

2. 「…近年來也有越來越多動畫是由…」，中，使用 More and more 來譯出越來越多，而 more and more，除了有加強語氣作用外，通常須用於進行式的句型上。

3. 「…有些是改編的，有些是原創的…」譯成 "Some of them are origins; some of them are adaptations."，要注意 Some...;some... 用法有兩種區別，一種用於特定範圍（不可數名詞）狀況下，一種則用於範圍不定（可數不可數名詞）的狀況。

前輩指點

　　相信現在有機會接翻譯工作的譯者，不管是專職或是兼差，大部分都是運用電腦或是其他 3C 產品來進行工作，少有用手寫方式來進行的，工作效率上其實要比以往「手寫」時代要高出很多，面對中英文語言用詞的轉換上，自然就少掉很多塗塗改改，句子順序、結構的修改痕跡。也自然少有筆跡潦草，如天書般難以辨認的窘狀發生。但有沒有可能哪天會突然有沒電腦可用，需要用手寫的狀況發生呢？

　　另外還有狀況是，現在很多文字工作者，習慣對著電腦思考，沒有電腦的話就無法思考並同步將思考組合過的文字直接輸入電腦中，要是哪天突然接到只能用傳統手寫交稿的案子時，有沒有本事讓自己不腦袋呈現空白並能寫出能辨識的文字，倒是可以稍微訓練一下，而不能整個放棄掉。就像當年筆者參加翻譯證照考試時，數個小時的時間在固定空間內，只能運用原子筆、手翻紙本字典來譯出規定範圍的譯文及答覆相關題目時，能否「寫」的出來，也似乎成為平日亦須著墨注意的方向了。有空時還是稍微練習一下用「筆」寫字，拿著筆寫字時訓練思考能力及文字重組能力，以備不時之需。字若能寫得漂亮，也能為自己接案加值。

主題 8
健康 8-1

 英中對照

Yoga, with thousands of years of history, may be taken as an alternative therapy. It provides another sort of supplemental medical care that appreciates nature outside of main stream medicine. It utilizes ancient and easily controlled techniques to assist the human body develop the potential for self-medication and self-regulation to achieve a balanced well-being. It has been found by many researches that Yoga brings a positive influence to maintaining good health.

People nowadays live in an environment with tension, pressure and pollution due to advanced technology and economic advancement, which has damaged the balanced human inner system and caused many chronic diseases and modern civilization diseases. More and more office workers who live with tension in their lives get certain illnesses in digestive system like Irritable Bowel Syndrome (IBS), especially females aged between 20 to 30 years old. There is no accurate examination for IBS so far, and the cause of the disease is not defined. It is supposed to be caused by Dysautonomia.

The best and most natural way to improve IBS is by practicing Yoga and meditation to release pressure, and it also enhances the stability of the autonomic nervous system by adjusting dietary habits.

There are two major yoga poses can be taken:

1. Plow Pose (Halasana)
*   Lie on your back with bent legs and your arms beside you, palms downwards.
*   As you inhale, lift your legs and hips upwards, keep feet bent, put knees on the forehead, move hands to the back and supports your hips and back with your hands, lift them off the ground with four fingers face the back and thumbs face upward.
*   Support the body with fingers and shoulders, move hands, shoulders and backs to let jaw get close to the collarbone, raise legs over the head till the toes touch the floor, push the floor with hands and look up, hold breath for 30 to 60 seconds.

2. Extended Side Angle Pose (Utthita Parsvakonasana)
*   From Warrior II pose (with right knee bent), bring the right elbow down to the right knee, inhale and raise the left arm up towards the ceiling and then exhale and lower the arm over the ear, making a straight line with the left side of your body.
*   Keep the right knee bent directly over the ankle, sink the hips down towards the floor, and reach the left fingers away from the left foot.
*   Breathe and hold for 3-6 breaths.
*   To release inhale and reach the left fingers up and back into warrior II or straighten the legs coming into 5 pointed stars.
*   Repeat on other side.

Dietary intake should be improved. We should increase the intake of fruit, vegetables, fiber, water and Lactobacillus and decrease allergens like eggs, milk, peanuts, corns, chocolate and stimulus like tea, coffee, soft drinks and cigarettes.

中文

　　有數千年歷史的瑜珈可被視為是一種替代療法，於主流內科醫學之外，提供另一種崇尚自然的補充醫學照護，運用古老且易於掌握的技巧，幫助人類發揮自身潛能，讓身體自癒並自我調節，達到平衡養生的目的。已有不少研究發現，瑜珈對於維護身體健康有正面的影響。

　　現代人拜科學、經濟發達所賜，處於緊張、壓力及污染環境中，使得一些人體主要官能運作系統的平衡被破壞，慢性病與文明病叢生，產生不少問題，在消化系統問題方面，就有越來越多久坐辦公室並且生活緊張的族群患有腸躁症，尤以 20~30 歲上下的女性居多。目前腸躁症醫學上並沒有準確的檢驗方式，也不知確切發生原因，但其實它應該算是自律神經失調引起的問題。

　　藉由瑜珈、冥想來紓壓，並在飲食上做調整來維護自律神經的穩定，是對腸躁症最好及最自然的方法。

有兩個瑜珈主要動作可採用：

1.　鋤式
- 雙腿曲膝，上半身趟臥在地板上，雙手放在身體兩旁。
- 吸氣，雙腿及臀部用力往上蹬起，雙腳保持彎曲，膝蓋放額頭上，雙手移至背部，四指頭朝背部，大拇指朝前扶住上半身。
- 用手指及肩膀撐地，移動手、肩膀及背部，讓下巴靠近鎖骨，穩住後將雙腳往後伸直，腳趾點地，雙手交握伸直推地，眼向上看，保持呼吸停留 30 秒至 60 秒。

2. 三角延伸式

- 從戰士二式（右膝彎曲），將右手肘下放至右膝，吸氣將左手臂向上伸至天花板方向，吐氣將手臂身高過耳朵，使身體左側成一直線。
- 維持右膝直接在腳踝上彎曲，臀部向地板下沉並碰觸左手指，左手指與左腳分開。
- 保持呼吸 3 至 6 次。
- 吐氣，左手指朝上還原戰士二式，或將雙腿伸直成五星式。
- 換邊重複做同式。

　　飲食攝取則需要改變。我們應該增加蔬果、纖維素、白開水、乳酸菌的攝取，減少攝取過敏原食物，如：蛋、奶、花生、玉米、巧克力，及一些刺激物，如：茶、咖啡、飲料和菸。

單字片語解釋

- supplemental　*adj.*　補足的、追加的
Increase in blood pressure might be attributable to supplemental consumption of a large amount of vitamin E.
大量補充維生素 E 有可能導致血壓升高。

- well-being　*n.*　康樂、安康、幸福
He works for the well-being of his family.
他為他家人的健康幸福而努力。

- chronic　*adj.*　長期的、（病）慢性的
She was suffering from chronic bronchitis.
她有慢性支氣管炎。

- digestive system　*n.*　消化系統
Mary does not maintain the digestive system of her body well.
瑪莉的消化系統沒有保養得很好。

- Dysautonomia　*n.*　自律神經失調
Long-term pressure is one of the causes of Dysautonomia.
長期壓力是自律神經失調的成因之一。

相關句型翻譯要點

1. 原「…於主流內科醫學之外，提供另一種崇尚自然的補充醫學照護，運用古老且易於掌握的技巧，幫助人類發揮自身潛能，讓身體自癒並自我調節，達到平衡養生的目的。」譯成 "It provides another sort of supplemental medical care that appreciates nature outside of main stream medicine. It utilizes ancient and easily controlled techniques to assist the human body develop the potential for self-medication and self-regulation to achieve a balanced well-being"。

2. 原「…在消化系統問題方面，就有越來越多久坐辦公室並且生活緊張的族群患有腸躁症…」譯成 "More and more office workers who live with tensional life in their lives get certain illnesses in digestive system like Irritable Bowel Syndrome (IBS), especially females aged..." more and more 可作形容詞或副詞，多用於進行式的句子中，作形容詞之後接複數名詞或不可數名詞，若作副詞用，之後則接副詞或形容詞。

⭐ 前輩指點

　　翻譯本身其實算是服務業，因此和所有服務業者所需遵循的原理是一樣的，而就工作邏輯而言，應該要「站在客戶的立場著想」。因為從顧客觀點來看，他們其實實質上是正要向他不認識的人花一筆錢，買一項先前從沒買過的服務，而他們並不瞭解如何進行，也不清楚該花多少錢、或是整個服務工作進行的內容及流程，如何進行才順暢、後續服務問題等等。

　　因此時供服務的譯者，就更應該對客戶適時提供專業建議，這些建議包含了：費用資訊、所需時間及參考資料、準時交稿及後續服務等資訊。在此建議為了讓顧客有回饋意見的機會，譯者也可以像其他服務業一樣，設計簡單問卷請客戶填寫，或是直接與客戶聯繫時請他們寫下一些話，以作為見證或是參考改進的方向。

　　譯者有這樣的意見回饋資料庫收集起來，等同於智庫一樣，就較能清楚明白該改進的重點從而加強，有進步才能有機會獲得更多翻譯案件，朝更專業的譯者之路邁進。

主題 8
健康 8-2

 英中對照

There are not only nutrients that provide energy for the human body but also nutrients which maintain the metabolism of the human body. Substances that provide energy mainly come from Carbohydrates, proteins and fats. Other types of substances; however, are less required. They are called micronutrients and come from dietary minerals and vitamins. There are different intake suggestions for individuals who have different life styles, workout levels or healthy conditions.

The Ministry of Health and Welfare, Executive Yuen has published new dietary guidelines (2011 version), which are based on physical activity intensity and calories consumption for age / sex, as followed:

Fruit: 2 to 4 portions

Vegetables: 3 to 5 plates

Whole grains: 1.5 to 4 bowls

Meat and Beans: 3 to 8 portions

Dairy: 1.5 to 2 cups

Oil: 3 to 7 teaspoons, 1 portion of nuts

For people who have special needs, it is important to adopt specific dietary care principles. Hypertension is positively correlated with Na (sodium) intake. The more sodium taken; the more hypertension is caused. Fatness is also a factor to causing hypertension; therefore, it is a focus of hypertension prevention to limit sodium intake and control weight. Every 1 gram of salt contains 400 milligrams of sodium, and we have to pay high attention to this.

It is important to obey the following principles:
1. To check blood pressure regularly.
2. To pay attention to weight and maintain it at an ideal level.
3. To limit sodium and oil in diet, but increase potassium intake.
4. To get sufficient sleep and rest. Do not be impatient and excited.
5. Do not smoke or drink alcohol.
6. Exercise appropriately.
7. Do not take baths or soak in extremely hot or cold water for a long time.
8. Prevent constipation with unobstructed intestines.

中文

　　人體所需的營養素不僅有主要提供身體能量，維持身體正常機能並構成身體細胞組織的蛋白質、醣類及脂肪，還有每日需求量較少的微量營養素，即維生素及礦物質。依據個人生活習慣、運動狀況與健康狀況的不同，對營養素的攝取，也有不同建議。

　　行政院衛生福利部依選擇自身生活活動強度、對照性別年紀查熱量需求、依熱量需求建議六大類飲食份數三步驟，公布每日飲食指南如下（2011年版）：

水果類：2-4 份

蔬菜類：3-5 碟

全穀根莖類：1.5-4 碗

豆魚肉蛋類：3-8 份

低脂乳品類：1.5-2 杯

油脂與堅果種子類：油脂 3-7 茶匙、堅果種子類一份

　　而針對身體擁有特殊情況的人，則更應該針對其情況而採取特別的飲食照護原則，如高血壓與鈉的攝取量有明確地關聯。鈉攝取量越多時，高血壓罹患率也越提高。同時，肥胖也是造成高血壓的因素之一，因此鈉量的限制與體重的控制是預防高血壓的重點。每一公克食鹽中含有 400 毫克的鈉，對於鹽的攝取，要特別留意。

以下注意事項更應切實遵守：

1. 定期檢查血壓。
2. 注意體重並維持在理想範圍內。
3. 食用限鈉、低油飲食，並增加鉀的攝取量。
4. 要充分睡眠及休息，不要焦躁激動。
5. 不要抽菸、喝酒。
6. 適度運動。
7. 不要用太冷、太熱的水洗澡或浸泡過久。
8. 經常保持大便通暢，預防便祕發生。

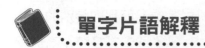

單字片語解釋

- nutrient *adj.* 營養的、滋養的
  Magnesium is the essential nutrient in plant growth.
  鎂是植物生長的營養要件。

- metabolism *n.* 新陳代謝
  The body's metabolism is slowed down by extreme cold.
  極寒可使身體的新陳代謝速度下降。

- carbohydrates *n.* 碳水化合物、醣類
  Food is made up of carbohydrates, proteins, and fats.
  食物由碳水化合物、蛋白質和脂肪構成。

- micronutrient *n.* 微量元素
  Flour and other grain products are main resources for Chinese to intake micronutrients.
  麵粉與其他穀物是中國居民微量營養素的主要來源。

- hypertension *n.* 高血壓、過度緊張
  Those who are overweight are candidates for hypertension.
  體重過重者易患高血壓。

- sodium　*n.*　鈉
Sodium and sulphur are highly corrosive.
鈉與硫酸腐蝕性很強。

- constipation　*n.*　便祕
It is helpful to eat more bran cereals, prunes, fruits, and vegetables for constipation.
多吃麥片、李子、水果及蔬菜是有利便秘的。

相關句型翻譯要點

1. 「人體所需的營養素不僅有主要提供身體能量，維持身體正常機能並構成身體細胞組織的蛋白質、醣類及脂肪，還有每日需求量較少的微量營養素…」中「不僅…還有…」我們使用 not only...but also... 句法來表示如下："There are not only nutrients that provide energy for the human body but also nutrients which maintain the metabolism of human body."

2. 句型「the 比較級 +the 比較級（越…越…）」很常見，可以是形容詞比較級，也可以是副詞比較級。第一句相當於條件從句。所以「鈉攝取量越多時，高血壓罹患率也越提高。」翻作英文即為 "The more sodium taken; the more hypertension is caused."

⭐ 前輩指點

　　對自由接案譯者來說，整個接案流程及翻譯服務進行方式，最好能有依據，才能保護雙方權益。譯者（服務的提供者）與客戶間需有文件或相關合約，來對雙方合作的案件，進行約定事宜，當中註明清楚相關細節，包括若提前解約或雙方未完成合約事項時的賠償作法，以保障雙方權益。雖然簽訂合約是件有點麻煩的事，但這個容易因為麻煩而常被自由譯者忽略的事，其實是對雙方的保障，不可不為啊！

　　其實所謂的接案合約，形式不拘，它也可以是份簡單的報價單（其中註明品項、服務單價、費用、總價、交稿日期、付款日期和方式、及其他雙方商定之事項）。只要請客戶確認無誤後再簽名回傳，就可作為憑證。此外，若客戶對於需要翻譯的材料有保密要求，亦可於合約中另外註明。

主題 **8**

健康 8-3

英中對照

Some children often grind their teeth during sleep, especially when they are in the period of growing replacement teeth. Bruxism actually represents the condition of poor health and bad living habits. The problems of health and life can sometimes be identified by bruxism. It is harmful for teeth. It makes teeth sensitive and unable to resist stimulants like cold, hot, acidity, and sweetness. It increases the chances of getting toothache, bleeding gums, and loose teeth if the teeth suffer from this for a long time.

The causes of bruxism from daily life is as followed:

1. Hyperphagia - It is common for children to have hyperphagia. Overeating increases the burden on the intestines and stomachs of children, especially overeating before sleeping. It, combined with indigestion, causes bruxism on children.

2. Over chewing - Long term working of masticatory muscles causes muscle fatigue and it leads to unconsciously chewing even when the teeth should be resting.

3. Mental stress – Long term mental stress in children also causes bruxism during sleep. The stress might come from exaltation during

play, especially before sleep. For children, music should be played or stories should be told for relaxation. Adults who have bruxism should pay more attention to this aspect.

The causes of bruxism from nutrition are as follows:

1. Parasites in bowels - Secretions and toxins from parasites stimulate the brain to shrink masticatory muscles and it leads to bruxism. This kind of bruxism usually occurs combined with vomiting and stomachaches.

2. Oral disease - Oral disease like chronic periodontal disease and irregular teeth causes bruxism. Mothers should take kids to get treatment for such disease; for example, kids should wear braces to correct irregular teeth.

3. Picky eater - Some kids are picky eaters and this leads to imbalanced nutrition. Masticatory muscles shrink unconsciously when they lack calcium. Children should overcome the problem of being choosy over food. Growing children must not be picky eaters.

Please do not ignore the issue of child bruxism. It is not a terrible problem and it can be eliminated once the cause is found. It, however, becomes a serious problem if it is not taken seriously.

中文

　　不少小孩子晚上睡覺時，總會磨牙，特別是在換牙時期。其實磨牙是一種身體狀況不佳，生活習慣不好的表現，因此有時透過磨牙我們可以察覺出身體與生活的問題。磨牙直接會對牙齒造成危害，使牙齒變得敏感且經受不住冷熱酸甜的刺激。長期下去容易發生牙疼、牙齦出血、牙齒鬆動等狀況。

磨牙的產生的原因在生活飲食上的有以下：

一、飲食過多積食—這種情況在小孩子身上容易發生。吃得太多，尤其是睡前吃得太多，會造成腸胃負擔，再加之孩子本身的消化不良就會導致磨牙。

二、嘴巴過度咀嚼—這種情況是由於咀嚼肌長時間的工作，造成肌肉疲勞，以致於在休息時仍然不自覺得咀嚼導致磨牙。

三、精神緊張與壓力—長期處於精神緊張之中，也會導致睡覺磨牙現象。對小孩來說壓力來自於玩耍時的過度興奮，尤其是睡前的過度興奮。因此對孩子來說，讓他聽聽音樂，給他講講故事放鬆一下。對磨牙的成人來說這一點原因應更加注意。

因身體營養有關的磨牙原因則有以下：

一、腸道存在寄生蟲—蟲子的分泌物和毒素刺激了大腦引起咀嚼肌收縮導致磨牙。如果是這種情況還會伴有嘔吐、肚子痛等症狀。

二、口腔疾病—比如慢性牙周炎、牙齒咬合不佳等。如果有像牙周炎這樣的疾病，媽媽應該及早帶孩子治療。像牙齒咬合不好的情況應佩戴牙齒矯形器來根治。

三、孩子挑食―挑食常會引起營養不均衡。如果缺了鈣等元素就會引起咀嚼
　　肌不由自主的收縮，造成磨牙。另外孩子一定要克服挑食，正在成長的
　　孩子一定不能挑食。

　　當發現小孩子磨牙時，請不要忽視，它並不可怕，只要找到問題所在，
應該就可以根除，置之不理的話，很有可能變成大問題，所以不能不注意。

 **單字片語解釋**

- bruxism　*n.*　【醫】磨牙症，夜間磨牙
  Mr. Wang's tooth is whittled down to stumps, due to bruxism.
  由於磨牙症關係，王先生的牙齒磨到只剩殘牙。

- stimulant　*n.*　刺激物、興奮劑
  Caffeine and nicotine are stimulants.
  咖啡因與尼古丁是刺激物質。

- Hyperphagia　*n.*　食慾過盛、飲食過多
  The diabetic patients exhibit the symptoms of hyperphagia,
  hyperposia and hyperuresis.
  糖尿病人出現多食、多飲及多尿症 。

- indigestion　*n.*　消化不良
  She is suffering from indigestion.
  她有消化不良症狀。

- masticatory　*adj.*　咀嚼的、咀嚼器官的
  Healthy teeth maintain the masticatory function well.
  健康的牙齒維持良好咀嚼力。

- exaltation　*n.*　興奮、得意洋洋

He was filled with a sort of exaltation for a moment.

他一時間突然興奮了起來。

- parasites　*n.*　寄生蟲

The lazy man was a parasite on his family.

那懶人是家裡的寄生蟲。

- vomit　*n.*　吐出物　*v.*　嘔吐

The mixture of drinks made me vomit.

那混和飲料使我嘔吐。

1

翻譯技巧

2

主題範例

相關句型翻譯要點

1. 「…磨牙直接會對牙齒造成危害，使牙齒變得敏感且經受不住冷熱酸甜的刺激。…」譯成 "It is harmful for teeth. It makes teeth sensitive and unable to resist stimulants like cold, hot, acidity, and sweetness." 此處兩個 it，皆為代名詞，代表磨牙這件事。

2. 「當發現小孩子磨牙時，請不要忽視，它並不可怕，只要找到問題所在，應該就可以根除，置之不理的話，很有可能變成大問題，所以不能不注意。」譯成 "Please do not ignore the issue of child bruxism. It is not a terrible problem and it can be eliminated once the cause is found. It, however, becomes a serious problem if it is not taken seriously." 當中的 however 有反而的意思，是一種語氣轉折的表達。

⭐ 前輩指點

　　從事翻譯，難免有些時候會遇到譯者本身超級不熟悉的領域或專業範疇，當前這種資訊時代，甚至都到雲端世紀了，運用相關的科技或資訊搜尋技術，相信最後一定能解決掉。不過，「一切都問 google 大神」，這種方式通常得花上一點時間，若是遇到的案件剛好是較趕的案子，恐怕這樣的方式會拖延到進度，不見得是適宜的解決方案。

　　就像旅遊有時會遇到的「認路」、「找路」問題一樣，本來每個人的喜好與傾向不同，處理的方式也不同，找路方法也就各異其趣。偏好自行 google 搜尋，循線慢慢搭配地景認路的就有點像是自由行旅者，享受著過程，並有可能在過程中，意外的再有其他方面的收穫，時間上較有可能避免不了延誤問題。另一種找路方式則是當街問當地路人，一些當地路人甚至就直接帶你到目的地了，更快找到路。

　　有些時候，譯者其實也不用花費太多時間在網路搜尋，或是在圖書館裡枯坐終日來釐清不熟悉領域的知識，直接找到當事人或是相關領域的專家，有可能一通電話或是見一次面，問題馬上解決，比先前還有效率。

1 翻譯技巧

2 主題範例

主題 **8**

健康 8-4

 英中對照

Uterine fibroid are one of the common tumors in woman. At least one-fifth of women aged above 35 developed uterine fibroids, and two-fifths of women aged above 40 develop it. The cause of uterine fibroid is so far unclear; however, it is possibly related to estrogen. Genetic factors and personal physique also affect it.

Most uterine fibroids are benign tumors. It is not necessary to have surgery unless there are the following symptoms:

• Obvious symptoms occurring like uterine bleeding, heavy periods, anemia, and micturition.
• Rapid growth during regular tracing examination.
• Abnormal growth after menopause.
• Infertility without other causes.

It is not necessary to have surgery for fibroids smaller than 5 centimeters because these symptoms are rarely presented. The decision on removing the whole uterus or not depends on the fibroid's size, fibroid's location, fibroid's numbers, patient's age, and the fertility status of the patient.

Women developing uterine fibroids are usually caught in a dilemma between surgical and non-surgical treatments. Fortunately, there is a new operation called HIFU introduced to Taiwan in 2015. This is a new medical procedure which destroys uterine fibroids through ablation without surgery. It does not lead to bleeding, and there is no need to take out the stiches after the operation. It is also called non-invasive surgery because there is no need to fast and no adhesion in the abdominal cavity after surgery. It helps the patients to effectively get rid of uterine fibroids.

HIFU is the abbreviation for high-intensity focused ultrasound. It applies high-intensity focused ultrasound to tissue which is transformed into heat. The fibroids are ablated after the treated area is heated to 60 degrees. The process does not damage the normal uterine tissue and the necrotic tissue can be gradually assimilated by the normal tissue. The symptoms will be eased when the uterine fibroids become smaller. There is no wound or pain, and patients can exercise freely two hours after the surgery and work as usual the next day. It is currently not included in the National Health Insurance Scheme and the cost is about NTD160, 000 to NTD180, 000. It is a new surgical option that has high-safety and low-risk.

1

翻譯技巧

2

主題範例

中文

子宮肌瘤是婦女常見腫瘤之一，估計 35 歲以上婦女，至少有五分之一有肌瘤，而 40 歲以上婦女，則有五分之二以上有子宮肌瘤。子宮肌瘤的成因目前尚未明確，但可能與動情激素有關，兼有個人體質與遺傳基因等因素相互影響。

子宮肌瘤大部分是良性腫瘤，除非有以下症狀，不然是是不會採取開刀治療的：

- 有明顯的不適症狀，如：月經量太大、月經期太長、貧血、頻尿等。
- 在追蹤檢查中，腫瘤日益快速變大。
- 停經後腫瘤反而更顯著變大。
- 長期不孕且無其他因素存在。

特別是小於五公分的肌瘤，大部分沒有症狀，就沒必要開刀。如果需要開刀，無論是只拿掉瘤，或是摘除整個子宮，也得視肌瘤大小、位置、數目，和患者的年齡、生育狀況做考量，才能適當決定。

罹患子宮肌瘤的婦女，常會在開刀不開刀間陷入掙扎，幸好台灣在 2015 年起引進了一種新手術，稱為「海扶刀」療法。這是一種不需要切開皮膚，就可以消融體內「子宮肌瘤」的新技術，不會流血、不需要拆線，不需要禁食，也不會造成腹腔內沾黏；因此又稱為「無創手術」，可有效幫助患者遠離子宮肌瘤夢魘。

　　海扶手術，是高強度聚焦超音波（High-intensity focused ultrasound, HIFU）的縮寫，以高強度聚焦超音波作用於組織，並轉化為熱能，使作用區域溫度到達 60℃以上，可使組織消融。治療過程不損傷正常的子宮組織，消融治療所產生的壞死組織可被正常組織逐漸吸收，使子宮肌瘤變小，達到減輕或緩解相應症狀。手術後約兩小時，就可以下床自由活動，隔天就可以正常工作，不會有傷口疼痛的問題發生。目前健保不給付此種手術，收費約在 16-18 萬元左右。是一種安全性高風險低的手術治療新選擇。

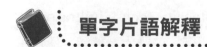

單字片語解釋

- uterine fibroid   *n.*   子宮肌瘤
  Uterine fibroids are the most common gynecologic tumors.
  子宮肌瘤是最常見的婦科腫瘤。

- tumor   *n.*   腫瘤、腫塊
  The third scan revealed a brain tumor.
  第三次掃描發現了腦腫瘤。

- estrogen   *n.*   【生化】雌激素
  There are different opinions for estrogen hormone therapy advice.
  目前對雌激素療法的意見尚不一致。

- benign   *adj.*   良性的、有益健康的、有利的
  Most of these tumors are benign.
  這種腫瘤大部分屬良性。

- anemia   *n.*   貧血症
  The doctors analyzed the blood sample for anemia.
  醫生分析了貧血的血液採樣。

- menopause　*n.*　更年期、絕經期

Women in Taiwan generally have the menopause between 45 years old to 51 years old.

台灣女性通常在年齡介於 45 歲至 51 歲間進入更年期。

- ablation　*n.*　消融、脫落

Electrical ablation is one of the surgical options for Liver cancer.

電燒法是處理肝癌的可行手術之一。

相關句型翻譯要點

1. 原「…至少有五分之一有肌瘤,而 40 歲以上婦女,則有五分之二以上有子宮肌瘤。」譯作 "At least one-fifth of women aged above 35 developed uterine fibroids, and two-fifths of women aged above 40 develop it." 使用分號連接兩子句,更能顯示出兩子句間的關聯性。

2. "It is not necessary to have surgery unless there are the following symptoms" 中 unless 是連接詞,意指「除非」,和 except if 及 if not 的意思相同,但不需搭配假設語法。當使用 unless 連接兩句時,句子 1 + unless + 句子 2,表示若「句子 2」不成立時,就會發生「句子 1」的狀況。

3. 原「…如果需要開刀,無論是只拿掉瘤,或是摘除整個子宮,也得視肌瘤大小、位置、數目以…」譯作 "The decision on removing the whole uterus or not depends on the fibroid's size, fibroid's location, fibroid's numbers..." 在此使用 (whether) or not,有「無論是…或是」的意思。

⭐ 前輩指點

　　翻譯從業人員，不管是公司固定編制內的全職翻譯，或是不在一般公司體制下的自由譯者，其實都與世界上任何工作一樣，絕對不是件不需投入體力、精神就可以輕鬆完成的工作，有意以翻譯為終身志業的朋友們，不管是因追求理想實現，或是現實維生而從事這份工作，也都該如同其他業別人士一樣，須保有職業道德意識，對自己所從事的工作切實負起責任的完成它。

　　不過在工作進行的同時，有時可能會有意想不到的突發狀況產生，如突如其來的重大疾病或意外，導致原訂進度有所延誤甚至無法繼續，這時就更考驗著除了專業能力外的處世應變能力了。這種層次的問題，就如同職場上大家老掉牙在討論的「做人？做事？」問題一樣，取捨之間，真的考驗著事主極大的智慧。就像上述的職業道德、合約精神與快爆的肝指數、白血球指數間的衝突，如何取捨？智慧啊！

主題 8
健康 8-5

英中對照

There is a trend for increased numbers of allergic rhinitis, sinusitis, and asthma patients currently. PM2.5 from air pollution might be the main cause for the health problem excluding seasonal and individual patient's factors.

PM is the abbreviation for particular matter, and it means the matter suspended in the Earth's atmosphere. PM 10 is a particulate matter with a mean aerodynamic diameter of 10 μm. PM2.5 is particulate matter with a mean aerodynamic diameter of or less than 2.5 μm.

PM is usually the main cause for poor air quality in Taiwan when the north-east monsoon prevails during autumn and winter. PM2.5 can easily enter the human body and be absorbed rapidly. The matter runs into the entire body through blood circulation and causes diseases. The impurities may cause asthma and affect and damage the tracheal mucosa which then leads to trachealis. Low air pressure makes chest tightness when it's foggy, and impurities including acid, amine, benzene and pathogenic microorganisms may cause cerebral hemorrhage. The conjunctiva is also easily affected and causes conjunctivitis. There are symptoms like tears, coughs, sneezes, runny noses, stuffy noses, sore throats, sleepiness and weariness when exposed to smog for a long time.

Smoggy weather impacts the respiratory system a lot, and it easily causes disease like acute upper respiratory tract infections and pneumonia. It is suggested that people decrease long term out-door activity and wear masks or goggles when the PM2.5 exceeds the norm.

Besides, traditional Chinese physicians believe "white food" that replenishes and promotes circulation is helpful for the respiratory system, and it is effective to maintain lungs in a good condition. It is suggested that people consume much more white food like pears, tremella, dioscorea opposite extract and lotus seeds to enhance the body's cleaning ability to ease illness caused by the haze.

1

翻譯技巧

2

主題範例

中文

近日過敏性鼻炎、鼻竇炎及氣喘患者有增加趨勢，除了季節與患者本身因素外，空氣污染造成的 PM2.5 細懸浮微粒，可能是造成民眾健康問題的最大成因。

PM 是 particulate matter 的縮寫，指的就是空氣中的懸浮粒子，其中直徑小於或等於 10 微米的懸浮粒子稱為可吸入懸浮粒子（PM10）；直徑小於或等於 2.5 微米的懸浮粒子稱為細懸浮微粒（PM2.5）。

在台灣，東北季風盛行的秋、冬季節，懸浮微粒往往是造成空氣品質不良主因。直徑小於 2.5 微米的顆粒物可以順利進入人體迅速被吸收，並進入血液循環，遍布全身，引發各系統疾病。雜質會引發哮喘，也會感染氣管粘膜造成損害，引發氣管炎。而起霧時氣壓低，容易感到胸悶，雜質中所含的酸、胺、苯與病源微生物等劇毒，會引發腦溢血。眼結膜也容易受感染導致結膜炎。長時間曝露在霾害中還會有流眼淚、咳嗽、打噴嚏、流鼻涕、鼻塞、喉嚨痛、睡眠不佳、嗜睡、疲勞等症狀。

霧霾天對呼吸系統影響大，容易引起急性上呼吸道感染、肺炎等疾病。因此當細懸浮微粒超標時，應減少出門與長時間戶外活動之外，出門時最好戴口罩或護目鏡。

此外，傳統中醫認為，偏重益氣行氣的白色食物，有益於呼吸系統，對肺有保養功效。因此建議多吃白色食物，如梨子、白木耳、山藥和蓮子等，增強肺的自我清潔能力，以緩解霧霾引發的不適症狀。

單字片語解釋

- allergic rhinitis　ph.　【醫】過敏性鼻炎
Patients with allergic rhinitis are more often affected by sleep disorders.
過敏性鼻炎患者更容易受到睡眠障礙影響。

- monsoon　*n.*　季風、雨季
Travelling is much more difficult during the monsoon.
雨季時旅行會比較困難些。

- prevail　*v.*　盛行、流行
Barbaric customs still prevail in the rural area.
偏遠地區仍盛行一些野蠻習俗

- impurity　*n.*　雜質
This impurity of water is harmful to humans' health.
水的雜質對人體健康有害。

- trachealis　*adj.*　氣管的
She is taking a surgery related to musculus trachealis-related surgery.
她正在動氣管相關手術。

1 翻譯技巧

2 主題範例

🔍 相關句型翻譯要點

1. 原「其中直徑小於或等於 10 微米的懸浮粒子稱為可吸入懸浮粒子
（PM10）；直徑小於或等於 2.5 微米的懸浮粒子稱為細懸浮微粒
（PM2.5）。」 譯 作 "PM 10 is a particulate matter with a mean
aerodynamic diameter of 10 μm. PM2.5 is particulate matter with
a mean aerodynamic diameter of or less than 2.5 μm."。

2. 原「此外，隔絕或避免接觸汙染源外，傳統中醫認為，偏重益氣行氣
的白色食物，有益於呼吸系統，對肺…」譯作 "Besides, traditional
Chinese physicians believe "white food" that replenishes and
promotes circulation is helpful for the respiratory system..."
besides 意思為是「除…以外還有…」，將後方的人／事／物「包含在
內」，用於「附加說明」，意思等同於 as well（也）或 also 及 plus（外
加）。

⭐ 前輩指點

　　筆者曾在接受移民的國家工作生活過一陣子，瞭解到在這些國家從事翻譯工作的話，會比在台灣本地多出比較多的其他相關翻譯接案機會，因為這些國家本身培養的當地語言翻譯人才大部分是不足的，它們的確很需要外來的技術人才來因應其本地需求。因此，在傳統培養翻譯人才管道─學校之外，通常會有相關單位以認證或檢定之類的方式來認定翻譯資格，因為在此需求的翻譯人才通常會處理的案件常與移民事務相關，或是有一定程度涉及法律效力，因此正式的專業能力認定也就相對重要。

　　曾經參加過相關認證考試的筆者，發現到法律、醫藥兩大主題為參加此類認證考試時，比較常出現的題目範圍，畢竟此兩大範圍乃是移民在生活中比較會需要服務及溝通的範疇，不少公部門會在醫院、法院、警局設立翻譯服務，因此若有意增加接案量，增加服務移民的話，此兩範疇主題的加強，倒也是必要的。通常，在移民國當地提供翻譯服務，可以拿到的薪酬平均也是優於台灣很多，這方向可供譯者參考嘗試。

Leader 052

解密中英互譯技巧：翻譯+英文寫作能力一次躍進！

作　　　者	黃瀅瑄 (Sandra Huang)
發 行 人	周瑞德
執行總監	齊心瑀
企劃編輯	魏于婷
執行編輯	饒美君
校　　　對	編輯部
封面構成	高鍾琪

內頁構成	華漢電腦排版有限公司
印　　　製	大亞彩色印刷製版股份有限公司
初　　　版	2016 年 11 月
定　　　價	新台幣 380 元
出　　　版	力得文化
電　　　話	(02) 2351-2007
傳　　　真	(02) 2351-0887
地　　　址	100 台北市中正區福州街 1 號 10 樓之 2
E - m a i l	best.books.service@gmail.com
網　　　址	www.bestbookstw.com

港澳地區總經銷	泛華發行代理有限公司
地　　　址	香港新界將軍澳工業邨駿昌街 7 號 2 樓
電　　　話	(852) 2798-2323
傳　　　真	(852) 2796-5471

國家圖書館出版品預行編目資料

解密中英互譯技巧：翻譯+英文寫作能力一次躍
進！ / 黃瀅瑄著. -- 初版. -- 臺北市：力得文
化，2016.11
　面；　公分. -- (Leader；52)
ISBN 978-986-93664-1-0 (平裝)

1. 英語 2. 寫作法

　　805.17　　　　　　105018392